TO MAKE THEM PAY

DI SAM COBBS #3

M A COMLEY

DEDICATION

Thank you to the wonderful Clive Rowlandson for allowing me to use his wonderful photography for the covers in this series. I'm glad I was able to squeeze Alpha in this one too. Happy 13th birthday, Alpha, you're an amazing dog.

ACKNOWLEDGMENTS

Special thanks as always go to @studioenp for their superb cover design expertise.

My heartfelt thanks go to my wonderful editor Emmy, and my proofreaders Joseph and Barbara for spotting all the lingering nits.

Thank you also to my amazing ARC Group who help to keep me sane during this process.

Thank you also to my good friends Alex and Claire for allowing me to use their names as characters in this series.

To Mary, gone, but never forgotten. I hope you found the peace you were searching for my dear friend. I miss you each and every day.

ALSO BY M A COMLEY

Caring For Justice (a 24,000 word novella)

Savage Justice (a 17,000 word novella)

Justice at Christmas #2 (a 15,000 word novella)

Gone in Seconds (Justice Again series #1)

Ultimate Dilemma (Justice Again series #2)

Shot of Silence (Justice Again series #3)

Taste of Fury (Justice Again series #4)

Crying Shame (Justice Again series #5)

To Die For (DI Sam Cobbs #1)

To Silence Them (DI Sam Cobbs #2)

To Make Them Pay (DI Sam Cobbs #3)

To Prove Fatal (DI Sam Cobbs #4)

Forever Watching You (DI Miranda Carr thriller)

Wrong Place (DI Sally Parker thriller #1)

No Hiding Place (DI Sally Parker thriller #2)

Cold Case (DI Sally Parker thriller#3)

Deadly Encounter (DI Sally Parker thriller #4)

Lost Innocence (DI Sally Parker thriller #5)

Goodbye My Precious Child (DI Sally Parker #6)

The Missing Wife (DI Sally Parker #7)

Web of Deceit (DI Sally Parker Novella with Tara Lyons)

The Missing Children (DI Kayli Bright #1)

Killer On The Run (DI Kayli Bright #2)

Hidden Agenda (DI Kayli Bright #3)

Murderous Betrayal (Kayli Bright #4)

Dying Breath (Kayli Bright #5)

Taken (DI Kayli Bright #6)

The Hostage Takers (DI Kayli Bright Novella)

No Right to Kill (DI Sara Ramsey #1)

Killer Blow (DI Sara Ramsey #2)

The Dead Can't Speak (DI Sara Ramsey #3)

Deluded (DI Sara Ramsey #4)

The Murder Pact (DI Sara Ramsey #5)

Twisted Revenge (DI Sara Ramsey #6)

The Lies She Told (DI Sara Ramsey #7)

For The Love Of... (DI Sara Ramsey #8)

Run for Your Life (DI Sara Ramsey #9)

Cold Mercy (DI Sara Ramsey #10)

Sign of Evil (DI Sara Ramsey #11)

Indefensible (DI Sara Ramsey #12)

Locked Away (DI Sara Ramsey #13)

I Can See You (DI Sara Ramsey #14)

The Kill List (DI Sara Ramsey #15)

I Know The Truth (A Psychological thriller)

She's Gone (A psychological thriller)

Evil In Disguise – a novel based on True events

Deadly Act (Hero series novella)

Torn Apart (Hero series #1)

End Result (Hero series #2)

In Plain Sight (Hero Series #3)

Double Jeopardy (Hero Series #4)

Criminal Actions (Hero Series #5)

Regrets Mean Nothing (Hero series #6)

Prowlers (Di Hero Series #7)

Sole Intention (Intention series #1)

Grave Intention (Intention series #2)

Devious Intention (Intention #3)

Cozy mysteries

Murder at the Wedding

Murder at the Hotel

Murder by the Sea

Death on the Coast

Death By Association

Merry Widow (A Lorne Simpkins short story)

It's A Dog's Life (A Lorne Simpkins short story)

A Time To Heal (A Sweet Romance)

A Time For Change (A Sweet Romance)

High Spirits

The Temptation series (Romantic Suspense/New Adult Novellas)

Past Temptation

Lost Temptation

Clever Deception (co-written by Linda S Prather)

Tragic Deception (co-written by Linda S Prather)

Sinful Deception (co-written by Linda S Prather)

PROLOGUE

"*R*ight, it's my round. What do you want this time, Ian?"

Ian rubbed his chin and then winked at the barmaid. "I'll have a vodka and tonic if he's paying."

The barmaid laughed, poured their drinks and took the money.

Reaching for his full glass, Brian downed half his red wine then let out an exaggerated sigh. "Jesus, the more I drink, the more I need to bloody piss. I'll be back before you can get another round in."

"No fear of that happening, it's your turn. Don't be long, I'm on a roll."

Brian slipped off his stool and staggered towards the toilet in the corner of the public bar, leaving Ian to contemplate their night out and the range of topics they had covered that evening. Everything from Brian's first disastrous shag to how he'd become a fisherman after spending two mind-numbing months stacking shelves at Tesco when he was a teenager, with little to no career prospects on the horizon.

His mate returned a few minutes later. On the way, he

almost toppled into a group of men sitting at the table close by. One of them got to his feet and pushed Brian towards the bar.

"Sorry, pal. Didn't mean to bump into you. It's the demon drink affecting me walking, innit?"

"If you can't handle your drink, then you should pace yourself, twat features. I've watched you down glass after glass. You're pathetic." The bearded chap looked over at the barmaid. "Cheryl, you need to stop serving him if he's already in that state."

"All right, Tyler, mind your own business, there's a good chap," Cheryl flung back.

He grunted and flopped back into his chair.

Ian rolled his eyes at the barmaid. "Don't worry, I'll get him home after this one. Sorry if we got you into any bother."

Cheryl waved away the suggestion. "Hey, I can handle myself, don't worry about me."

Ian nodded. "I can tell. Come on, Bri, let's be having you. Sup up and I'll walk you back to your boat."

"I'm not about to let that tosser spoil my evening."

"Neither am I. Hey, enough is enough, the last thing we want is any form of trouble."

Ian finished his drink, and Brian followed suit.

"Thanks, Cheryl, you're the best barmaid this side of Scafell Pike," Brian slurred.

"Get him outta here before he makes a drunken pass at me." Cheryl winked at Ian.

Ian jumped off his stool and hooked Brian's arm around his shoulder. "Come on, Twinkle Toes, let's get you home and tucked up into bed."

"Aww... you're the bestest friend ever, but even I have my limits. I refuse to sleep with you, if that's what you're asking."

"Geez... nothing could be further from the truth."

Ian found the whole experience challenging. Once the fresh air hit them on a blustery April evening, Brian's staggering seemed to intensify to the extreme. Ian pulled the man tighter to get a firmer grip on him and upped his pace.

"Hey, why the race to get home? I could do with another drink."

"When you're back on the boat, mate. Play fair, stop fighting me and lend a hand, will you?"

Brian wrenched out of his grasp. "I said leave me alone. I'm going to call into the Wheelhouse and have another one before I go home, and there's nowt you can do to stop me."

Ian made sure the coast was clear first and then slammed a fist into Brian's flushed face. His legs gave way beneath him. Ian had to be quick; he caught him before Brian hit the ground, knowing that if he didn't, he wouldn't be able to get his drunken friend on his feet again.

Now which boat is his again? Ah yes, the one at the rear of the jetty. "Come on, mate, not far to go now."

"You hit me. Why?"

"Because you're being a grade-A plonker and time is getting on. I need to get myself home as well before midnight."

"Why? Got a bird waiting in satin sheets for you ready to screw, have ya?"

"Pack it in. You know me, I steer clear of the opposite sex, they're more trouble than they're worth."

"Ain't that the truth?"

"Come on, Bri, lend a hand. I'm knackered here."

"Sorry, me legs have gone, pal. All I want is me bed, I do."

"You'll get it soon enough."

Ian steered his friend down the jetty towards the fishing boat at the end. His strength deserted him when he tried to haul Brian aboard the vessel. "Give me a break, you're gonna need to do better, either that or I'll drag you aboard."

"I'm doing me best here. It's harder than you think to stay focussed. Putting one foot in front of the other has always been a weakness of mine, especially when I've downed a few bevvies."

"Try harder or I'm going to leave you to it."

Brian stood upright and swayed a little. He concentrated on climbing over the side and fell onto the deck. Ian followed him onto the twenty-eight-foot craft and heaved Brian up onto his feet again. He searched Brian's pockets for his keys and opened the door.

"Shit, are you going to make it down there?" Ian stared at the six steep steps leading down to the cabin.

"Aye, I'm used to it. Get out of me way." Brian shoved Ian to one side and put a foot on the top step, only his second foot failed to connect with the next one, and instead, he tumbled down the rest and ended up at the bottom, groaning in agony. "Jesus, what happened?"

Ian shook his head. "Are you okay?"

"Get me to me cabin. I'll sleep it off."

Ian struggled to right his friend, his strength waning considerably by this point. "You're a heavy lump."

"I'm not. I'm the same weight I was when I was eighteen and started on the boats."

Ian wasn't about to argue with him. He yanked Brian up on his feet and pushed him along the narrow corridor to his cabin. He threw open the door and shoved him on the bed. "Right, if you think I'm undressing you, you've got another think coming. I'm outta here. Are you going to be all right?"

"Yeah, you go. Thanks for your help, mate. Just shut the door on your way out."

"I'll do that. Goodnight, Brian. I have a feeling you'll be asleep before I get off the boat."

Ian craned an ear. Brian's snoring and lack of verbal

response confirmed his suspicion. He left the boat, closed the door behind him and walked back up the jetty.

THE INTRUDER OPENED the door and crept down the steps. He searched the boat for the cabin and found it a few seconds later. The boat was small, not really big enough to get lost on. He dumped his black holdall on the bed next to the man who was out cold. Opening the bag, he withdrew several instruments and positioned them alongside the man who was snoring loudly.

He undid some gaffer tape and placed it over the man's mouth. Brian's eyes shot open, but he didn't move.

"Now don't be an idiot. Stay still and it'll all be over soon."

Brian tried to speak, but the tape did its job to suppress his words.

"Shut the fuck up."

Brian's head tilted to the side, his gaze drifted to the instruments on the quilt beside him, and he pissed himself.

The smell filled the cabin. "Jesus, you're a disgusting excuse for a man."

Brian's muffled response was ignored by the intruder. He picked up a large meat hook and dug it into Brian's right arm. Brian yelled, or tried to, and he attempted to clamber off the bed. The intruder straddled him and rearranged the balaclava over his head; he'd contemplated bringing a second one to put over Brian's head but then ditched the idea in favour of wanting to see the fear in his victim's face during his torture.

Blood oozed out of the wound and seeped into the yellow quilt cover. The intruder kept the momentum going. Another instrument was chosen, a long-bladed knife, and he dug it into Brian's chest several times. Brian's eyes widened and then stayed wide as death came calling.

Shit! Where was the fun in that? Why did I finish him off so quickly? Dumb idiot!

He wiped the equipment on the quilt and was in no hurry to pack up his instruments of torture. With the chore carried out, he left the victim and proceeded to search through his belongings. "Might as well see what I can take. It's not like he'll be needing anything where he's going. May he rot in Hell."

On the dresser were a couple of good watches. He popped them in his pocket and searched the drawers for anything else that might take his fancy. He sighed, disappointed, picked up his holdall and kicked the victim's dangling leg as he passed. "So long, arsehole. It was nice getting to know you." Laughing at his wicked sense of humour, he made his way back up on deck. He checked the coast was clear. It was almost midnight, so he presumed everyone would be tucked up in bed by now.

He jumped onto the jetty and ran the length of it on tiptoes—that was an effort he hadn't anticipated.

Brian had it coming. The killer felt no remorse as he drove away from the crime scene.

CHAPTER 1

"Good morning, Sonny." Sam Cobbs tried to fend off her dog's slobbery kisses, but it was pointless. His tongue always managed to find a way through her fingers. She grabbed him, wrestled him into position beside her and rested her head against his. "You're in trouble now." He licked the side of her face, and she snuggled into her golden cockapoo's fur. "Grr... I should have made an appointment at the groomer's, you're in dire need of a hair-cut, buddy."

She noted the time on the clock: six-ten. There was no point in her trying to sleep now. She'd lain awake most of the night, her mind reeling with different scenarios on how to improve their lives—hers and Sonny's. That's all she had now, since Chris, her husband, had decided to walk out on them. One argument too many, who could blame him? She'd gone through a gamut of emotions in the two weeks since his unexpected departure. Anything and everything from feeling guilty to anger emerging and eating away at her. She was done with all that now. It was his loss. If he no longer wanted to be a part of her life, there was little she could do to change his mind. She couldn't force him to stay with her. Would she want him under the same roof if it was grudgingly? No, they were better off going their separate ways.

What she couldn't forgive, was him not telling her face to face that he was running out on her and not being in touch since. She had no idea where he was. Even his parents didn't know. They had been devastated when she'd told them the truth. She'd stirred up a hornet's nest there as well.

She had vowed that she wasn't going to dwell on the matter any longer. It was time for her and Sonny to get on with their lives. Since Chris's departure, she'd spent more time than ever at the park with Sonny. He was her sole attention now. Of course, her frequent visits to the park had also meant she'd bumped into Rhys more and more as well. Their friendship had grown considerably now that Chris was out of the picture. Although, nothing major had happened, other than them sharing the odd kiss here and there. Even then, the kisses had only consisted of a quick peck on the cheek most of the time.

She threw back the quilt, covering Sonny in the process. He shot off the bed and wound himself around her legs on the way to the bathroom. "Hey, pack it in, that is if you want to get an early morning walk?"

He sat and inclined his head from side to side. She loved the very bones of him. She ruffled his head and continued her journey to have a shower. When she emerged, Sonny was nowhere to be seen. She called his name, and he came bounding into the room, carrying his octopus cuddly toy. Sam made a grab for it, and he bolted out onto the landing. "You cheeky bugger. Let me get dressed."

A quick check out of the window confirmed her suspicion that it was drizzling. "Great, I'm going to get wet again. Is there any point in drying my hair?"

Sonny moaned behind her.

"Yeah, my thoughts exactly. Good job I've just bought you that waterproof coat, matey."

TWENTY MINUTES LATER, and Sonny was tearing around the park, chasing after the squirrels.

Her heart raced while she combed the area for Rhys. She mentally kicked herself for acting like a hormonal teenager. *I'm still a married woman. Rhys is a kind, handsome man, but it doesn't alter the fact that I'm still wearing Chris's ring on my left hand.* Doing her very best to put her latest admirer out of her mind, Sam picked up a stick and threw it for Sonny. He bounded after it then veered off towards the stone bridge at the other end of the park. "Sonny, come back. Don't you dare run off and make me late for work."

A female jogger passed her. "They certainly pick their moments, don't they?"

Sam shrugged and shook her head. "He's a sweetheart, usually. Not sure what's got into him today."

The woman smiled and carried on jogging. Sam trotted after Sonny and found him paddling in the river on the other side of the bridge. She couldn't help but laugh; what was the point in getting upset? Any other time she would be encouraging him to have a paddle. "Come on, numpty, out you pop. Let's get you home and dried off before I take you next door to Doreen."

Sam swallowed down her disappointment at not seeing Rhys and attached Sonny's lead. Back at home, after towel-drying Sonny and then blasting him with the hairdryer just to make sure he didn't have any excess water hiding in his coat, she gathered the bag of food and toys she had prepared the evening before and nipped next door.

Doreen was a friendly lady, a widow who had lost her ex-navy husband over two years ago. She spent most of her days at home. Sam hadn't really had much to do with her until recently. One quick chat over the fence when they were both hanging out washing one day and that was it, a firm friendship had developed between them. In passing, at the beginning of the previous week, Sam had mentioned her dilemma, about Chris leaving and that Sonny would now be at home by himself most of the day. Doreen quickly volunteered her services. She had a cat named Ginger, even though she was black, who always came to visit Sonny in the back garden. They had hit it off more or less right away, so when Doreen had offered to look after Sonny during the day, Sam had jumped at the chance to leave her pup in her new friend's company. The only stipulation Doreen had given was that she wouldn't be able to walk Sonny during the day as she was awaiting hip replacement surgery. That didn't matter to Sam. She adjusted her alarm clock, getting up at the crack of dawn most days, to ensure Sonny received an extra-long walk every morning before she headed off for work.

The kindness of strangers never failed to amaze her some days, especially after dealing with the worst side of people's nature during her working day at the station.

"Good morning to you. And how is my precious new housemate today?" Doreen ruffled Sonny's head.

"He's been a little bugger. Decided to take a dip in the river this morning. I've dried him off, so you needn't worry."

"Dogs can be so unpredictable, can't they?"

"Damn right they can, especially this rascal. Here's his stuff. I've marked up his meals, just in case I'm late back. Who knows what will turn up today?"

"Leave him with me. We're going to have a blast. Don't worry your pretty head about a thing, he's safe with me, you know that, Sam."

"I'm so grateful for all you do for me. I'm not sure what I

would do if you hadn't offered to care for Sonny during the day."

"Get away with you, it's a pleasure. Never a chore to spend the day with this little beauty, I can assure you."

Sam quickly glanced at her watch. "Right, it's time I was going. You've got my number, if you need to speak with me during the day, don't hesitate."

"I have, it's sitting by the phone. Now shoo… be off with you and go and catch all the criminals of Workington."

She chuckled. "I doubt if I'll ever manage that even if I spent the next fifty years on the force."

"It won't stop you putting in the extra effort, though, knowing you."

"I'm glad you have faith in me."

"Oh, I do. Come on sweetie, let's get you settled."

Sam bent to kiss Sonny, but he ran into Doreen's house. She stood up again and stared at her neighbour, gobsmacked. "I don't think he's going to miss me one iota."

Doreen's mouth turned down. "Don't think of it that way, just be grateful that he's settled well and isn't pining for you all day. We should both be grateful for that."

Sam turned towards her car and called back, "You're not wrong there. I'll see you later. Thanks again, Doreen."

"You're always welcome, as is Sonny. Don't fret over him. He and Ginger get on great and spend most of the day cuddled up together."

"Good to know." Sam waved and hopped behind her steering wheel. She smiled at Doreen and drove off.

During the twenty-minute drive into Workington, her mind was full of guilty questions: why had her marriage failed? Why had Chris taken off, without thrashing out their problems with her first? Why did Sonny have to be the main one to suffer in all of this? Not that he appeared to be suffering at all, being looked after by Doreen. He was Sam's therapy, the one thing keeping her sane.

After pulling into her designated parking spot, she locked the car and made her way in through the main entrance. A tap on the shoulder had her clutching a hand to her chest. She spun around to confront the person. "What the f...? Jesus, Bob, you scared the crap out of me."

"Sorry. You were miles away. I called you half a dozen times."

"I heard you," she lied. "It's my prerogative, as your senior officer, to ignore you when I feel the need to."

He took a step back, and his mouth gaped open for a second or two. "What the hell? Why would you ignore me of all people?"

It was her greatest pleasure in life, to wind him up. He was standing before her, his eyes swimming with emotion.

"Have I done something to offend you that I don't know about? Or do you just have a downer on men in general at the moment?"

"Come on, we have work to attend to. We haven't got time to spend around here all day trying to make sense of your insecurities."

He mimicked a goldfish out of water. She turned her back and did her best to hold in the laughter threatening to escape as she ascended the stairs. Some of the team were already sitting at their desks. DS Claire Owen, their resident computer expert, was trawling through the system. Claire was the mainstay of her team, highly reliable, who put as much into her role as Sam herself did. She was deserving of her recent rise up the ranks to sergeant level.

"Morning, Claire. How are Scott and the children?"

"Still keeping me on my toes, boss."

"You wouldn't have it any other way, though, would you?"

"You've got that right. How are you?" Claire whispered.

Sam wrinkled her nose. "Good days and bad, but I keep plodding on. Don't worry about me, Mum always says I'm a born fighter."

"I hope things work out for the best for you soon."

"Thanks." Sam moved on to the next desk and spoke to Liam O'Callahan. "Morning, Liam. Any further forward with your wedding plans?" She had a soft spot for Liam, one of the younger members of the team, always eager to put ideas forward during complex cases.

"It's all in Sarah's hands, boss. I chip in when she wants my opinion on something eating away at her, but most of the time she seems on top of organising everything."

"Typical man, taking a step back," she ribbed him.

"Not at all. I just know my place in the relationship."

Sniggering, she walked towards her office. "Umm... a coffee would be nice, Bob, thanks for asking. I'll be sorting through the post. Give me a shout when the rest of the team show up."

Bob chuntered something under his breath and made his day worse by catching his ankle on a chair leg en route to the drinks' station. He entered the office a few seconds later and placed the coffee on her desk. "You don't deserve that."

She sat back and stared at him. "Don't I? Why's that then?"

"For being unnecessarily mean to me downstairs. For your information, I don't suffer, and have never suffered, from insecurities."

Sam inclined her head. "If you say so, partner. Now run along, we've all got a great deal of paperwork to attend to after solving our latest case."

He mumbled something indecipherable and closed the door behind him.

She smiled. It was the first time she'd felt the old Sam returning to near normal after feeling down since Chris had left. *Does that mean I'm over him? Does it heck!* Her team had been great throughout, especially Bob, despite her intent to wind him up. They had all given her the space she had needed to get on with her life, without the need to ask her every five minutes how she was or if there was anything they could do for her. That's what she needed, to get her life back, and if Chris didn't want in on the action going forward, then it was his loss, not hers.

It was fifteen minutes later that she realised Bob hadn't come to collect her. She straightened up the post she'd been dealing with and left her office. Bob was standing by her door, his hand raised, ready to knock.

"Oh, I thought you'd forgotten about me."

"Like that's possible," he grumbled. "Umm... Alex showed up in distress, we've been sorting him out."

Sam glanced over at Alex Dougall's empty desk and frowned. "Where is he?"

"I told Oliver to run him to the hospital."

"Why? Come on, Bob, spit it out."

"He got attacked by a gang of youths on the way into work. They set a German Shepherd on him. Covered in bruises and bite marks, he is."

"You should have called me. Is he all right?"

"Pretty shaken up for a big man. He'll be fine once the doctors have seen to him at A and E. Don't tell me I shouldn't have sent him to hospital."

"Why would I say that?" she challenged.

Her partner's broad shoulders raised and then fell. "The mood you've been in lately, I wouldn't put it past you."

"Sorry, I didn't realise I'd been that grouchy."

"Ha. Take my word for it, you have."

"All right, let's leave it there for now, Bob." She moved to the front of the room. "How is everyone getting on with the files they were tasked with?"

"Most of us have completed them, we're just waiting on Alex to finish his off," Claire was quick to respond.

"I know it's asking a lot, but would you mind picking up the slack, Claire? There's no telling how long he's going to be out of action."

"Consider it done." Claire left her seat and searched through the files on Alex's desk and took them back to her own.

"Do you need a hand, Claire?" Sam asked.

She flicked through the files and shook her head. "I should have these done and dusted within a few hours."

"Great stuff. Give me a shout if you hit any problems."

"I'll be all right, boss."

The phone rang on her desk in the office, and Sam sprinted to answer it. "DI Sam Cobbs, how may I help?"

"Ah, the lady herself. This is Des Markham, DI Cobbs. If you're not too busy, I'd like you to join me out at Whitehaven Harbour."

"Why so formal, Des? And is that a note of sarcasm in your tone I'm detecting?"

"Moi? Never. Well, are you about to grace us with your presence? The sooner the better, if you don't mind, I'm eager to get the body back to the mortuary. I have the PMs stacking up and if I don't get ahead of the game soon, I'll be swimming in bodies back at base."

"Is that supposed to mean something? Was there a pun in there that has passed me by?"

Des groaned. "Never mind. My sparkling wit is obviously wasted on you."

"Probably. I apologise. What do I have to look forward to?"

"What are we talking about? In your personal life, or are you asking what awaits you here?"

What are you doing to me? Just answer the damn question, Des.

She smiled, hoping Des would pick up on her smiling at the other end. "What awaits me, is that better?"

"Ah yes, it's always a good idea to speak with clarity, I find, especially in our line of business."

"Absolutely. So? I'm waiting."

"Would you believe? A dead body!"

Sam closed her eyes and shook her head. She was used to the pathologist being obstreperous when it suited him. "I'll see you soon." She ended the call and slipped on her raincoat. "Bob, it looks like we have yet another case to keep us occupied. We'll be in touch with the details soon, team. In the meantime, do your best to wrap up all the lingering paperwork at hand, in our absence."

Bob followed her out of the incident room and down the stairs. "Where are we going?"

"Whitehaven, to the harbour. Don't ask me anything else, Des was in one of his awkward moods."

"There appears to be a lot of that flying around lately."

Sam stopped mid-descent and faced her partner. "Meaning?"

"Umm... I was just saying," he stuttered.

"Except you weren't, nothing could be further from the truth. What is wrong with all of you? Have you intentionally been planted in my life to piss me off?"

Her partner scratched the fluff on his chin, his brow furrowing into deep crevices. "What are you going on about?"

She didn't bother elucidating and continued on her journey out to the car, her partner huffing and puffing with frustration behind her.

The traffic was easier than she had anticipated, and they arrived at the location within ten minutes. Des was in the process of issuing instructions to his team, his assistant, Vanessa, nodding eagerly by his side.

"Well, get to it. Vanessa, ensure my instructions are carried out to the letter, or it will be your arse I'm kicking if things don't go according to plan."

"Of course. Yes, Doctor Markham. I'll get on it right away. Come on, people, let's get cracking now."

Des spotted Sam and Bob arrive. "Ah, I see you're here at last. Well, what are you waiting for? Get kitted up."

"Efficient and as bossy as ever with your staff, I see," Sam stated.

"I like to keep them on their toes. An efficient team is a successful one, I'm sure you're aware of that, Inspector."

"I am. Although I tend to hold back from wiping the floor with them."

He tipped his head back and let out a demonic laugh. "As if I'm doing that. You have a lot to learn about me, Inspector." He dipped inside his van and extracted two white suits packed in plastic. "Time is getting on."

She decided it was best not to push things. She and Bob pulled on their suits and followed Des from the edge of the harbour down the jetty to a boat at the end.

"I take it we're going on board?" she asked.

"You're correct in your assumption. After all, that's where the body is. Do you have a problem with that, Inspector?"

Sam cringed, and her heart rate escalated. She had a phobia about being in confined spaces, it had haunted her since she was a child. In the past, she had avoided travelling on any type of boats. She smiled. "Not at all. Lead the way."

They paused to fasten their footwear coverings, and then Des showed them down the steep steps, along the narrow corridor and into the cabin. Sam's gaze was immediately drawn to the man lying on the bed. The scene was a bloody mess. The victim had several open wounds covering different parts of his body. The quilt beneath him had soaked up his blood.

"Nice," Bob whispered beside her.

Sam wafted away the stench of alcohol. "Hardly. Do you have any idea how the wounds were made, Des?"

"Not yet. My guess would be that something sharp was used but with a certain degree of force."

"As in something was swung and aimed at him?"

"Possibly, I'll know more when I can get access to the wounds properly during the PM."

"I'm taking it the use of the gaffer tape prevented the man from crying out during the attack."

"I'd say that was stating the obvious," Des replied, tilting his head enquiringly at her.

"Sorry, thinking out loud. Did the attacker come on board when the victim was asleep? I'd say that was an unlikely scenario, considering he's fully clothed. Maybe an unscrupulous individual saw the state he was in and followed him home."

"The latter seems the most likely. Alcohol, and vast amounts of it, were definitely consumed, judging by the bodily fluids the man has exuded since his death."

"Not a pleasant smell," Bob chipped in, his nose wrinkling because of the gross stench filling the tiny cabin.

Sam swallowed down the bile rising in her throat through not only the stench but the fact she was feeling the walls closing in around her. "Any idea when this happened?"

"My estimation would be between twenty-four- and forty-eight-hours max."

"Who found him?"

"A friend. He came aboard, thinking the victim was ill as he hadn't taken his boat out for a day or so. Raised the alarm as soon as he saw him." He pointed to the corner of the room and a pile of vomit. "That's what he brought up."

Sam puffed out her cheeks. "Nice... not. What you're telling me is that we know who the vic is, yes?"

"Yes, he's a Brian Coltman. He owns this boat and he's a fisherman."

"So he works and lives on the boat. And the friend is where?"

"He needed to get to work for an important meeting." Des dug out a card from inside his paper suit. "I told him you'd be wanting a word with him ASAP. He said to give him a call to arrange a time to speak with him."

"He said *what*? His friend is murdered and he casually goes on with his day as if nothing has happened? Geez, some people need to get a life."

"Sounds like he has one to me," Bob said.

She glared at him, and he had the sense to cast his eyes down to the floor.

Des held his arms out to the side in the tiny space. "I'm just passing on the message. Not sure there was an ulterior motive for him not hanging around, if that's what you're getting at."

"I wasn't, but thanks for the insight. Okay, going back to the murder scene, I suppose it's pointless asking if you have found any trace evidence on the body."

"It would be, yes. Nothing so far. We're going to do a thorough search before we move the body."

Nodding, Sam asked, "No sign of any weapons or instruments used lying around—that's too much to hope for, right?"

"Grasping at straws, I'd say. No sign of anything. Whoever the killer was, I suspect he arrived with his weapons and ensured he took them with him."

Sam shrugged. "So what *can* you give me at this early stage, Des, anything?"

"Not really, except that possibly some of the injuries might have been caused by some form of hook. Clearly, that's conjecture at this stage."

19

"What makes you say that?"

"Although the attack and force were substantial, a couple of the wounds appeared to have been carried out with precision."

"How can you tell?"

Des took a step forward and pointed to a wound in the victim's right arm. "A smallish hole here. Like I said, it's supposition for now until I can get a closer look back at the lab."

"I understand. Do you think the hook might have been a fishing hook?"

"Possibly. I've got one of my guys searching the equipment on board at the moment to see if he can find anything that fits the bill. However, I still maintain my first thought, that the attacker likely brought his items of torture or weapons with him."

"Mind if we have a nosey around down here and in the wheelhouse? See if we can find an address book with his next of kin details?"

"Go for it. Maybe his friend will be able to fill in the blanks, once you see him in person."

"We'll see. I'd rather have a root around if it's all the same to you?"

"Feel free."

Sam and Bob left the cabin and went back up on deck. She headed towards the small wheelhouse midway through the vessel. Pulling on a pair of latex gloves, she crouched and searched two cupboards off to the side of the wheel. There was a lot of paperwork to trawl through but no address book, not that she could see.

"Do men use address books?" Bob peered at the mess she'd made on the floor.

"I don't know, do you?"

"Nope. Any addresses I need I put in my contacts on my

phone. I think all blokes would do the same. Don't you do that?"

"And what if you lost your phone?" Sam fired back the quick retort.

"Ah, then I suppose I'd be up shit creek. But then... Abigail always notes things down..."

His voice trailed off, and Sam glanced over her shoulder at him. "What, in her address book? Goodness me, what are you men like?"

"All right, there's no need to have a go at me. Anyway, it's not like we don't know who the victim is, plus we'll be having a chat with his mate later, won't we? So all's not lost."

She skimmed the business card Des had given her. "The sooner we speak to Warren Podger the better. In fact, I'm going to contact him now." She fished out her phone and stood, leaving the mess on the floor. "You could put your gloves on and tidy that lot up for me."

He tutted. "How come I get all the crappy jobs?"

"Hello, this is your senior officer talking."

He chuntered some expletives, snapped on his gloves and got down on his knees while Sam placed the call.

"Yes, hello there, I'd like to speak with Warren Podger if he's available."

"Who's calling?"

"This is DI Sam Cobbs of the Cumbria Constabulary."

"Ah yes. He told me to expect a call from a police officer. He wanted me to ask you to call back this afternoon. His diary is full all morning, you see."

"He can't squeeze in a five-minute chat between appointments, is that what you're telling me?"

"Sadly not. He travels between his appointments."

"Then he can speak to me via his phone en route, can't he?"

21

"Mr Podger is a very busy man, Inspector. His journey time is taken up revising his notes for the next meeting."

"I don't have time to argue with you about this. All right, perhaps it would be better if he rang me at his earliest convenience, how's that?"

"I'll pass the message on. Good day, Inspector."

She jabbed the End Call button and let out a disgruntled groan. Bob appeared beside her.

"No luck, I take it?"

"No. What is wrong with people? Surely he would know the importance of slotting in an early meeting with us?"

"We're not off to a good start with this case, are we?"

"Nope, at least we have the vic's name so we can do the necessary digging for now."

"And what else?"

Sam looked across the harbour at the small crowd gathered beyond the cordon uniformed police had put in place. "We start asking around. See if anyone either knew Coltman or saw anything that would be of interest to us."

"Want me to call for more bodies to lend a hand?"

"Makes sense to me."

Bob rang the station, his voice in the distance as Sam's thoughts drifted a little. She peered the length of the jetty, searching for any sign of cameras. She thought she spotted one outside one of the shops on the harbour and set off.

"Hey, where are you off to?" Bob called after her.

"I'll be right back."

She hopped onto the jetty, stripped off her protective shoes and clothing and tucked them into the waiting black sack. She then trotted back up the jetty to the gift shop. The bell tinkled above the door. A tiny woman with round glasses perched on the end of her nose looked over them at her.

Sam produced her warrant card and introduced herself. "Hi, sorry to disturb you. I'm DI Sam Cobbs."

"Ah, I thought you were with the police. You have that air of authority about you."

Sam chuckled. "I see. Okay, as you're probably aware, we're dealing with a major crime scene on one of the boats in the harbour."

"So I heard. Dreadful to think that poor young man has lost his life."

Sam's interest piqued to another level. "Did you know the victim?"

"Brian? Yes, always in here having a natter when he saw me alone. He told me once that I reminded him of his grandmother. She was barely five feet in her stocking feet, slightly taller than me. I believe that was the only similarity between us. Funny how something like that can spark a friendship, isn't it?"

"You knew him quite well then?"

"I suppose so." Her eyes teared up, and she dabbed at them with a lace hanky. "I'm sorry. I told myself I wasn't going to get upset again. Sobbed like a baby first thing, I did. He was such a lovely man. I shall miss his cheerful face around here."

"Have you known him long?"

"Around six or seven years. Since he bought the boat and started going out in it. He was short of money at the time. I thought he was getting thinner by the day so I used to pop next door to the café and buy him a couple of rounds of bacon sandwiches. He wasn't the type to take people for granted, he appreciated the kind gesture, and we became firm friends after that. Once he got back on his feet and the money started to roll in, he insisted on repaying my kindness. Took me out for a posh dinner at a fancy hotel up the road. A wonderfully kind man. They broke the mould when they made him, I can tell you." She dabbed at her eyes again.

"Sorry, I didn't catch your name."

"It's Elsie Minter."

"May I call you, Elsie?"

"Why not? Everyone else does around here."

Sam smiled at the older woman whose voice was strained with emotion. "I'm so sorry for your loss. What we're trying to ascertain is if Mr Coltman had any family in the area."

"Ah, let me think. During one of our many conversations, I seem to recall he mentioned his father lived in Workington. I'm not sure how close they were. I'm thinking not so close, not if he didn't talk about him that much."

"Do you happen to know his name?"

Elsie shook her head. "Sorry, even if he did tell me once, I can't for the life of me remember what it is. Hopeless, aren't I?"

"Not at all. We'll find him, I'm sure. Did Brian have a girl-friend or was he married?"

"Oh no. He's had a few girls over the years, nothing I would class as long-term relationships. I suppose once he showed them where he lived, they backed off. You've seen it. Not exactly the Ritz, his little boat, is it?"

"No, it's not. I suppose comfortable enough for a young man to call home, but yes, I couldn't see any females taking to it, that's for sure."

"Shame really. Although he never said, I always got the impression that he was keen to settle down with a nice young lady."

"It's a pity. By the sounds of it, he seemed a nice, caring young man. You mentioned his father, what about his mother?"

"Oh no, she's long gone. By that I mean, she tootled off and left him with his father when he was quite young."

Sam's interest turned up a notch. "Did he say why?"

"No, he clammed up when I tried to get it out of him. I

didn't want to push him, to do anything that would spoil our friendship, so I felt it was best left alone."

"Did he become sad or angry when the subject arose?"

"Hard to tell really. Maybe a little of both. I know that doesn't help but it's the best I can give you, sorry."

"That's fine. Maybe I'll get the facts from his father when I see him. What about friends in the area, did he have many?"

"Oh yes, he used to go out most nights with one friend or another. He was a typical sailor in that respect, liked nothing better than to finish the day with a drink."

Makes sense, considering he reeked of alcohol.

"Do you know if he stayed local when he drank?"

"Yes, all the pubs in the area knew him, I believe. He spread the love around, so to speak. A smashing boy, I really can't believe he's gone. I don't think my heart will ever be the same. He was one of those people you instantly got attached to, if that makes sense?"

"It does. Well, I'm determined to find out what happened to him and get justice for him."

"Good, you hear of so many crimes going unsolved nowadays. Hard to believe when science has come so far over the years, you know, with the likes of DNA profiling et cetera."

"You're aware of police procedures?"

"I think everyone is these days, what with all the true crime shows on TV. My late husband used to be a Scenes of Crime Officer as well, before his untimely death in an accident around four years ago."

"Oh no, how awful. Did he work in the area?"

"Yes."

"I probably knew him in that case."

"Tony Minter, you may well have done."

Sam suddenly felt awkward about the situation. After clearing her throat, she asked, "The reason I'm here is because I noticed you have a camera pointing at the harbour. Please tell me it's in good working order?"

"It is. It was Tony who ordered me to install it. Not enough CCTV in this area, he said."

"I agree with him. I don't suppose you have it working at night, do you?"

"Yes, twenty-four hours a day. Oh, I see what you're getting at. You think my camera may have captured the person responsible for Brian's death, is that it?"

"Or at least give us an approximate time of his death. At the moment, the pathologist isn't a hundred percent sure when the incident occurred."

"Very well, let's see what we can find then. Would you like a cuppa while we search through the disc?"

Sam beamed. "Sounds like a good idea to me. Why don't you point me in the direction, and I'll prepare the drinks while you set up the equipment?"

"Ah yes, there's nothing like a bit of teamwork to get a job done, is there? That was my Tony's motto, always helped me out around the house, he did. He wasn't one of those chauvinist pigs who liked to leave everything for me to do."

"You must miss him."

"That, my dear inspector, is an extreme understatement. Genuine soulmates we were; from our very first date, we knew we were meant to be together. Engaged within a month and walked down the aisle before our six-month anniversary."

"How wonderful. A true fairy tale romance."

"Indeed." Elsie sought out Sam's left hand and held it up. "I see you're married, dear. It must be hard being an exceptional copper and a doting wife. Excuse me for being forward, I can tell you're a true professional by the way you speak to people. You have a caring nature, it oozes from every pore."

"Hush now, you'll have me blushing. Sadly, my husband and I are going through a rough patch."

"Oh, I didn't mean to pry. Do you think you'll be able to work things out?"

"I wish I could answer that. The truth is, I can't. He walked out on me a couple of weeks ago and hasn't bothered to get in touch since."

"Oh my, that's terrible. You poor thing. Tell me to keep my nose out, but was it on the cards?"

Sam hitched up a shoulder and exhaled a long, slow breath. "I've gone over it a thousand times in my head. I suppose the warning signs were there but I'm guilty of ignoring them and concentrating on my job. It probably didn't help buying a house that needed renovating either. I think it was a slippery slope that just gained momentum. Hark at me, I'm sorry for burdening you with my woes, that was never my intention."

"I can tell when someone is desperate to air their troubles. You're a prime example. Never apologise for speaking openly and from the heart. Bottling things up, letting them fester, will only eat away at you in the long run. Now I'm guilty of teaching you how to suck eggs, aren't I?"

"Not at all. I appreciate hearing another person's perspective, an outsider's point of view at that."

"Haven't you spoken to anyone, dear? A friend or a colleague perhaps?"

"No, I haven't really had the time. There again, I wouldn't want to burden them either. Everyone has been through hell and back during this pandemic, the last thing I would want to do is pile extra pressure on their shoulders, sharing my problems."

"Oh, no, you really mustn't think that way. I'm certain your true friends would be appalled if you kept this from them, I assure you. Now, come on, let's get that cuppa, and if you feel like crying on my shoulder while we trawl through the footage, don't hold back."

Sam shook her head. "I'm fine, truly I am. In dire need of a drink, though."

Elsie pointed out where the 'entertaining area' as she put it was, and Sam got to work making two strong mugs of tea. She usually drank coffee but thought the change might do her some good in the old woman's company.

"Here you are. How are you getting on?"

"I've gone back to Monday evening. I haven't come across anything as yet. Oh, wait, what do we have here?" Elsie poked a finger on the rim of her glasses to push them back and pointed at the screen. "Yes, that's Brian. Blimey, he does look the worse for wear."

"Do you recognise the man holding him up?"

She examined the image lit up by a nearby streetlight as they walked past and then shook her head. "No, I can't say I do. You think that's the guilty party? Seems an outlandish idea to me if he's assisting him here."

"Hmm… maybe it was a ruse. Perhaps the man made out he was friends with Brian, got him on board the boat and then put his vile plan into action to finish him off."

"Do the villainous deed? My, I would never have come to that conclusion after seeing him help Brian on the camera. Oops, Brian is so far gone here. They appear to be laughing, don't they?"

Sam scratched the side of her face. "You're not wrong. I agree, it doesn't seem logical, but experience tells me that there are unscrupulous human beings out there who make a point of preying on the vulnerable."

"And no one is more vulnerable than a drunk who is trying to get home."

"Correct. Let's watch it a little more, make a note of what time the man leaves. And then I'll rewind it and see if I can get a better picture of him to print off. Maybe one of your neighbours might recognise him if I show the picture around."

"If we get a decent image. So far I haven't seen anything that might be suitable."

Holding up her crossed fingers, Sam kept her focus on the screen. What surprised her was the fact that the man appeared to leave a matter of minutes later. In her mind, that wasn't nearly long enough to carry out the vicious assault she'd witnessed on the victim.

"Poor Brian, to think he trusted that man and he let my young friend down in the cruellest way imaginable." Elsie stretched out an arm to switch off the machine just as a man in dark clothing, carrying a holdall, entered the bottom of the screen.

"Wait! Who's that?"

Elsie gasped and took a step back. "Oh no, someone up to no good by the look of things. Do you think he's the culprit?"

Chewing the idea over along with the inside of her mouth, Sam nodded. "To me, it seems a more likely prospect."

Elsie took a sip from her mug. They continued to watch the screen. After a while when nothing happened in the frame, Sam gave the instruction for Elsie to fast forward a little.

"Let's see what this brings us."

"Stop!" Sam shouted. The man reappeared ten minutes later, again carrying his holdall. He passed by the shop and tugged the peak of his cap down to cover his face. "He was aware of the camera."

"You think? Dearie me, could we be looking at the killer here?"

"Highly possible, I reckon. Can you do me a favour and

run me off a copy, Elsie? Would that be okay? Do you have a spare disc available?"

"Of course I do. I'll get on to it now. I wouldn't want to hold you up longer than necessary." The older woman shuddered. "Damn, feels like someone just walked over my grave. How shocking to realise the camera my adoring husband told me to put in has captured an image of a killer." She rubbed her hand between her breasts.

Sam noticed the colour drain from the woman's cheeks and pulled the chair forward. "Here, take a seat, you don't look so good. Are you all right, Elsie?"

"Honestly, I don't know. I suppose it's the shock. I have a burning sensation in my chest."

"As in you think you might be sick or do you think it's more serious than that?"

Elsie plonked herself into the chair and stared up at Sam. "I can't tell you. All I know is one minute I was feeling fine and the next, well, the only way to describe it is I feel like death warmed up. As though the Grim Reaper is knocking on my door."

"Oh bugger, don't say that. Let me call an ambulance for you."

"Nonsense. They've got enough to do without bothering with the likes of me. I'm sure I'll feel better soon."

"Do you want to tell me how I go about copying the disc and I'll take over?"

"Yes, it's simple really. Put the other disc in, line up from where you want to make the required copy and press the Record button."

A few minutes later and the task was complete.

Sam patted Elsie on her forearm. "How are you feeling now? The colour seems to be coming back in your cheeks a little."

"I'm sure I'll be okay. Let's face it, at least I'm still able to breathe, unlike poor Brian."

"There is that. I hate to leave you if you're feeling poorly, though. Is there anyone I can call to come and sit with you? Another shop owner or a family member?"

"I'll be fine. I'm returning back to normality quicker than I could imagine. You get off and do what you need to do. Here…" She picked up a pen and scribbled her phone number down on a slip of paper. "Call me if you decide you want to talk about your situation. Sometimes bending a stranger's ear can be a better outlet for some folks."

"You're very kind. I wish I could hug you, but the current rules are telling me that wouldn't be wise for either of us."

"The thought was there. You're a special lady, Inspector. Ensure you live your best life and be happy, that's my motto nowadays, since Tony's passing. I just wish we'd had more years together. We were both due to retire this year. I've decided to keep this place running for a while yet. What else am I going to do? Sit at home, getting bored all day and every day?"

"Not necessarily. We live in a beautiful part of the world. You could be out there exploring the area. I plan on doing the same when I retire."

Elsie became thoughtful and nodded slowly. "You know, I think you're right. Maybe I'll be a daredevil and take on the Wainwrights Walks challenge, what do you reckon?"

Sam giggled at the thought. "Crikey, you'd have to build up your fitness levels to take that on. I'm not sure I have all of the fells in me; maybe I'll tackle a few but definitely not all of them."

"Ah yes, I suppose I said it without considering the conse-quences on these old legs of mine. Anyway, I'm prattling on, holding you up. You go. I'll have my drink and shut up shop for the day. So don't go worrying about me, and don't forget to pick up the phone if you need someone to talk to."

"You're too kind. I think you're doing the right thing after losing such a good friend. You stay there, I'll see myself out." Sam ejected the disc and placed it in the plastic case. "I'll get this replaced for you."

"Nonsense. It's my gift to you in the hope that you find and punish the culprit."

"You have my word that I'm going to do my very best."

"I'm sure you will. It's been a pleasure spending this time with you. Wishing you every happiness in the near future. Oh, and if you don't mind me saying, I think that husband of yours is nuttier than a fruitcake. Maybe you're better off without him if he can't be bothered to tell you he's all right."

"Maybe. Take care, Elsie, you're a lovely lady."

The woman's cheeks flared up at Sam's words. She turned and left the older woman sitting in her chair and walked out of the shop. Out of duty, Sam nipped next door to have a quick word with the woman in the optician's. She asked if she knew Elsie. The woman was a similar age to Elsie, and she said they often went for a coffee together. Sam quickly ran through what had occurred and asked the woman if she wouldn't mind keeping a close eye on her neighbour.

The woman gasped. "Of course I will. That's dreadful news. I knew we had a police presence here today, but I had no idea why. If we can be of assistance, don't hesitate to ask."

"I will." Sam held up the disc. "I think we've got enough footage to be going on with for now. Do you have a camera installed outside?"

"Yes, we do."

Sam went over to the window and looked up. "Ah, it's pointing in the same direction as Elsie's so would likely pick up the same images."

"That's a shame. I feel as though we've let you down."

"Don't worry about it. I'll give you a shout if I change my mind and need extra evidence for some reason. Thanks for agreeing to keep an eye on Elsie, I'll be going now."

"I'll nip over there as soon as the latest customer comes out from seeing the optician."

"Thank you." Sam left the shop and surveyed the other ones in the area to see if any of them had any cameras fitted. Sadly, they didn't.

"Everything okay?"

Sam's heart all but leapt into her mouth. She spun around and slapped her partner on the arm. "Do you have to creep up on me like that?"

"I didn't. It's not my fault you were in a world of your own."

"I wasn't. If you must know, I was surveying the area."

He pointed at the disc in her right hand. "What's that?"

"What does it look like?"

"If you're in one of your moods, I can take my enquiring nature elsewhere, it doesn't bother me."

"Sorry, I didn't mean to take it out on you. You're quite within your rights to be short with me. The shop next door, the camera picked up Brian staggering home with a friend, the friend departing a few minutes later, and then someone dressed all in black showing up. That someone was carrying a holdall, likely full of torture weapons."

"Piece of piss now we've got him on disc then, right?"

"Think again. The person kept his head down, he was wearing a cap. I think he realised where the camera was. Yes, he walked past it but he did everything he could to avoid being recognised."

"Shit! You think he was goading us? Knowing that we'd probably seek out the footage?"

"Nailed-on certainty."

Bob's gaze drifted back to the victim's boat, bobbing around in the water as a sudden breeze got up.

"I see the extra bodies have arrived. Have you issued them with instructions?" Sam asked.

"Not yet. That's why I tracked you down. I wondered if you wanted to have a word with them."

"Why not? Okay. Let's get this over with. Call them all together at the end of the jetty, far enough away from the crowds so we're not overheard."

"I'll do that now. Won't be a tick."

Sam watched her partner march back towards the new arrivals. Once they were all gathered, Sam made her way over to them and said, "Okay, what we need you guys to do is ask around. Check with the other boat owners, see if anyone either heard or saw anything on Monday night, that's when the incident occurred." She waved the disc around. "I have the proof someone dressed all in black arrived to do the deed at around eleven forty-five. I want to know if anyone saw the perpetrator either arrive or leave. We also have evidence of Brian Coltman, the victim, coming home around fifteen minutes or so before his attacker showed up. He was staggering a lot, obviously inebriated. He was accompanied by a friend. This friend ensured Brian got home safely and left a few minutes later, possibly ten minutes before the killer arrived. Again, I want to know if anyone in the area either saw Brian and his friend here or possibly in a nearby pub. Any questions?"

The officers all shook their heads and split up.

"What do you want us to do next?" Bob asked, kicking a stone into the water.

"Let's hang around here for an hour or so, see what comes back from the enquiries. In the meantime, I want to stroll around the harbour to see if any other shop owners can help us out. First, I need to get a photo of the victim, preferably not one of him dead before you ask."

"As if I would? Let me see if he's got any social media pages going."

"Good idea. Let me know what you find out." Sam drifted around the harbour, contemplating where Brian and his pal might have come from that evening. Had they been involved in a possible confrontation? Had the person been that upset with Brian, they then followed him home to punish him? It seems questionable but still something we need to check out. What about the bag? Was it premeditated?

Sam had returned to the shops and was working her way through questioning the owners when Bob came looking for her again.

"I think we've got something," he said in one of the doorways.

"Thanks for your help," Sam said to the young woman she'd been speaking to in one of the charity shops. She joined her partner outside. "What's up?"

"One of the neighbours just came back to his boat. He said that Brian usually drinks at The Wheelhouse. I asked if he was there Monday evening, but he couldn't tell me. I thought I'd nip over there and ask the manager. What do you reckon?"

"Is it far? You know this area better than I do."

"Just around the corner, the bloke confirmed it."

"Let's go then."

"Want to go on foot or take the car?"

"Knowing how lazy you are, we'll take the car. Always better to have it to hand in case we need to go elsewhere in an emergency."

"Trust you to think like that."

CHAPTER 2

They walked back to Sam's car, and Bob directed her to where he thought the pub was located a few streets behind the harbour. "I told you it wasn't far, we could have walked it, taken the shortcut and got here in half the time."

"Okay, no need to rub my nose in it. So, you were right for once in your life." She threw him a smug grin and got out of the vehicle.

"You're going to regret having a dig at me one of these days when I'm no longer around to take the flack."

She stopped and wrenched on his arm. "What are you saying?"

"Nothing concrete, just issuing you with a warning."

"You wouldn't ditch me as a partner, Bob, would you?"

He shrugged and continued towards the main entrance of the small pub. The outside was decorated with an array of hanging baskets filled with winter pansies and emerging spring bulbs. It proved to Sam that the manager or owner of the pub cared about their punters and drawing in new customers. A sign of the times, in the current climate? The

36

only time she visited the pub off duty was when she met up with her parents for lunch on a Sunday. Maybe that was down to Sam being tight with money during the renovations. Anyway, she and Chris had found it far cheaper to drink at home during the pandemic. She shook her head, trying to rid herself of the image of the husband who had deserted her. Bob caught her in the act.

"Something up? No point saying it's nothing, I can feel the tension oozing out of you."

"Nope, I'm fine. Let's get this over with."

"If you're sure. You know I'm always here if you need a chat, don't you?"

"I do. Even if you do like to wind me up about ditching me."

"I was kidding. You used to have a sense of humour not so long ago."

Sam strode past him and muttered, "Like I have anything to laugh about right now, let alone smile about."

"Whose fault is that?"

She swiftly turned to face him. Her partner knew he'd done wrong; his teeth were sinking into his bottom lip, and his eyes were firmly closed.

"How dare you? What are you insinuating, Bob? Let's have it, a nice open conversation for a change."

"I… umm… sorry. I shouldn't have…"

"Opened your mouth before engaging your brain, is that what you're trying to get out? I agree. For your information, it's not my fault my hubby chose to walk out on me, no matter what either you or anyone else thinks. I wish I knew why he took off, the truth is, I don't. So stop putting the onus on me, got that?" She prodded him roughly in the chest.

"Ouch! That hurt."

"It was damn well supposed to."

"I apologise. You know what a big mouth I have at times. Am I forgiven?"

He twisted his lips and crossed his eyes.

All her anger dissipated in a flash. She gently punched his upper arm. "You're such a goon. Not sure how I'd get through the day without you by my side. So if you're thinking about jacking it in, I'm forbidding it. Who else could replace you and brighten my day the way you do?"

"Blimey! That's a turn-up for the books, next you'll be telling me you love me like a brother."

Sam's cheeks heated up under his intense gaze. "Well, I wasn't going to say anything but…"

She could tell Bob was embarrassed because he pulled another couple of goonish faces which made her laugh. "Right, let's get back to work, eh?"

"Sounds good to me. I think one major confession from you is enough for one day."

Chuckling and feeling like a heavy load had been lifted off her shoulders, Sam entered the pub and made her way to the bar. There were a few early punters sitting around. One old man with a beard was feeding a packet of crisps to his Jack Russell who was down by his side, begging. Sam had to bite down hard on her tongue to prevent herself from tearing a strip off the owner for feeding his dog fatty foods, judging by the paunch the dog was carrying; she doubted if it was a one-off event either. *Mind back to the case in hand, girl, you can't tackle some forms of stupidity.*

She approached the bar and held up her warrant card for the barman to study. "Hi, I'm DI Sam Cobbs, and this is my partner, DS Bob Jones. Are you the owner or manager?"

"I run this place, Jeff Adamson. What's this about?"

"We're making general enquiries about a Brian Coltman, do you know him?"

"Of course I do, he's one of my regulars. Done something wrong, has he?"

Sam slotted her warrant card back into her coat pocket. "Umm… actually, Mr Coltman died a few days ago."

The man's hands dropped onto the bar as if to steady himself. "What? May I ask how?"

"We believe he was murdered, although I can't go into detail."

"Bloody hell. That's shocked the bloody life out of me, that has."

"Can I ask when you saw him last?"

His head tilted back, and for a few seconds his gaze settled on the smoky ceiling above, a sign of bygone days when heavy smoking was allowed inside this pub. "When was it now? Monday, no, I think it was more likely to be Sunday. When did he die?"

"Possibly Monday evening. We know he'd been out drinking. Did he come in here that night?"

"No, he definitely didn't come in here. It was really quiet, I would have remembered."

"You're certain it was Sunday he was here, then?" Sam asked.

The man lowered his head to look at her. "Yes, thinking about it, I'm certain it was."

"Do you know what other pubs he frequents in the area?"

"Take your pick, love… sorry, Inspector. There are around five within walking distance of the harbour—that's where he moored his boat, not sure if you're aware of that."

"We are. How well did you know him?"

"Well enough. Can't believe anyone would knock him off, such a decent chap. The type to offer a helping hand if you needed one. Even helped me out behind the bar when one of the girls had called in sick."

"Did he have a lot of friends in the area?"

"Sort of. A lot of acquaintances I'd call them, or probably drinking buddies would be more accurate. In other words, he tended to flash his money around, got a lot of hangers-on lingering near him whenever he set foot in this place. I had to have a word with him, tell him to pack it in and that some of the gits were using him, but he wouldn't listen to me. Said he didn't mind, wanted to share his good fortune around."

Sam and Bob glanced at each other, then Sam asked the barman, "Good fortune? Was he flush? After a big win on the lottery or something similar?"

"No, well, not as far as I know. He did well with his business, didn't have many overheads living on that boat of his, so I suppose he had a lot of what you'd call disposable income."

"Ah, I see, therefore he splashed the cash around without a care in the world."

"You've got it. In my opinion, it's never a wise thing to do in a pub, you only attract the wrong type of people to be your drinking buddies. He wouldn't be told, though. Said I was driving him nuts because I was always going on about it. At the end of the day, I was looking out for the poor bugger. You get to see all sorts standing behind this bar all day, I can tell you."

"You were right to try and warn him if this is the result. Would you be able to give us any names in particular? You know, the ones who appeared to only be after his money?"

"Why? You think one of them killed him?"

"It's a line of enquiry we need to consider."

"Is that what folks do? Kill people just to get a few extra pints in their bellies? Seems a tad over the top to me."

Sam shrugged. "It's not unheard of. If someone is desperate enough for money to pay off debts, you'd be surprised what they're capable of."

Jeff mulled over the idea. "Look, I wouldn't want to get

any of my punters into bother just because they tapped Brian up for a few extra pints during their time in here. If you see what I'm saying?"

"How will that sit on your conscience if someone else gets murdered?" Sam bit back without thinking through her question first.

"Now wait just a minute. There's nothing the matter with my conscience. I think you're going about this the wrong way. You're expecting me to drop the names of a bunch of lads who, in my opinion, were only guilty of tapping a bloke up for a few drinks. How do you suppose that's going to affect my conscience if you end up arresting one of them for murder?"

Sam was intent on standing her ground with the now irate owner. "It shouldn't make any difference to you one way or another if the person turns out to be the killer, should it?"

"I'm not in the business of fitting someone up for a crime they may or may not have committed."

"All we're asking for is possible names. I assure you, we're not in the 'business of fitting people up' as you put it. What I need to do is have a word with these people to eliminate them from our enquiries. There's nothing sinister going through my mind, I can promise you. If the evidence were there, then we would proceed with making an arrest; if no evidence came to light, then we would walk away. I don't know what type of coppers you've dealt with in the past but, believe me, that's not how I perform my job. My partner can vouch for me if you ask him."

"Yep. All we're trying to do, mate, is find the killer and prevent them from taking another life."

Jeff shrugged. "I can't help you, and no, that's not me trying to piss you off. Most of the punters I only know by their first names. I take it you'll be expecting me to supply surnames, addresses and phone numbers after that, right?"

Sam smiled. "Not necessarily. Any detail, no matter how insignificant you believe that information is, could help our enquiries."

Jeff heaved out a sigh and cast a glance over his shoulder at the counter close to the till. Seeing what he was after, he took two steps backwards and grabbed a small pad and a pen on which he proceeded to write down information. Returning to his position, he handed a sheet of paper to Sam. On it were three names: Colin, Mark and Dan.

"And these people regularly hung out with Brian?"

"That's right. They all live within walking distance of the pub, but as far as any other info goes, that's it. Sorry and all that."

"It is what it is. What about jobs? Any idea what type of jobs they have?"

Jeff ran a hand around his beard. "My mind has gone blank, sorry."

Sensing they were getting nowhere fast, Sam decided to call it a day. "I'll leave you my card. If you should hear any kind of gossip or if anything comes to mind after we leave, don't hesitate to get in touch. I can't emphasise enough what finding this killer would mean to this community, Jeff."

"Yeah, I realise that. If I hear anything worth knowing, I'll call you, I promise. Brian didn't deserve to die, especially not like this anyway."

"I'm glad we agree on that point."

Outside, Sam asked her partner, "Can you bring up the other pubs in the area?"

Bob tinkered with his phone and shifted position so they could both view the tiny screen. "Two over this way, the rest dotted around within a few roads."

"I can't believe there are so many in this area. Let's try the two closest first and work our way back from there."

"Makes sense. I reckon he would have probably visited the closest ones in all honesty, you know, within staggering distance of the harbour."

"I agree. The Golden Hind it is then."

They jumped back into the car and drove the short distance to the next pub they'd chosen. A blonde barmaid welcomed them as they entered.

Sam showed her ID. "DI Sam Cobbs, and my partner, DS Bob Jones. We're making enquiries about a possible customer of yours."

"Oh, right. I'll do my best to help. What do you need to know?"

"Do you know a Brian Coltman? He's a fisherman and lives on his boat in the harbour."

"Hang on, yes, I think so."

Bob got out his phone and angled it towards the barmaid. "We're not sure how old the photo is, but it might help you recognise him."

"Yes, that's the Brian I was thinking about. Been up to no good, has he? Always came across as a cheeky chappie to me."

"Umm… when I said we're making enquiries, it's for a murder inquiry."

"What? Are you telling me he's *dead*?"

Sam sighed and nodded. "Sadly yes. What we're trying to do is form a picture of his final hours. Have you seen him lately?"

"Oh gosh, how awful. He was in here a few days ago."

"Can you be more precise? What day?"

"I think it was Monday. Tuesday is my day off. Yes, was definitely Monday."

"Was he alone or in here with a friend?"

Her eyes narrowed. "No, he was with another fella who I

don't know. Brian is a regular, at least two to three times a week most weeks."

"Can you give me a description of the man he was with?"

Bob withdrew his notebook when Sam asked the question.

"I heard them chatting. He was called Ian, if that helps."

"It does. Anything else?"

"Brown hair, quite short. He appeared to be neatly presented. By that I mean he wore trousers and a jacket, not matching as in a suit—not the usual jeans-and-T-shirt brigade is what I'm trying to say."

"Interesting. What about his physique and other characteristic features, anything coming to mind?"

"Clean-shaven, no beard which is a rarity these days. Quite handsome. I noticed how good his skin was, I remember that. Compared to Brian's, I suppose him being out at sea in all types of weather is bound to have some effect on his complexion at the end of the day."

"Height and approximate weight?" Sam ploughed on.

"Blimey, now you're testing me. Around the six-foot mark, maybe an inch or two either side, very slim. Light-brown hair, quite short, sorry, I've told you that already. He seemed a businessman type, if there is such a thing."

"Perfect. And you're sure you've never seen him before?"

"Definitely. I thought he must have been a friend visiting Brian from out of town. He seemed really pally with him. The conversation was natural, they were winding each other up, which made me presume they knew each other well. Maybe I'm wrong about that; it's the impression I got, listening to their conversation anyway."

"Did you pick up on anything interesting?"

"Such as?" the barmaid asked.

"Anything at all. What about what the guy did for a living perhaps?"

"I can't recall, sorry."

"Were they in here long?" Sam's gaze rose to the back of the bar. "Is that a camera?"

The barmaid clicked her fingers. "I'm such an idiot at times. Yes, of course it is. They were sitting in those seats right there, so the camera will have definitely picked them up."

"Can you take a look for us?"

"Sorry, I'm a technophobe. The boss deals with that sort of thing. He's seeing to a delivery at the moment, he shouldn't be too long. I can get him to run through the machine with you."

"That would be great."

"Can I get you a drink while you're waiting?"

"Two coffees, if you don't mind. White with one sugar."

"Why don't you take a seat, and I'll bring them over?"

Sam and Bob drifted to the corner. From there, Sam had a great view of the rest of the bar and the door as well.

The barmaid brought two mugs of coffee and set them on the table. "I've had a word with Matt, he's just setting up the machine now. He said he'll give you a shout when he's ready."

"Brilliant. Thanks so much."

The barmaid left them to it.

"Sounds hopeful. If we can get an ID on this guy, I reckon we're halfway to solving the case," Bob murmured. He blew on his drink and then took a sip. "Nice coffee. Mind you, anything is better than the shit we have at our disposal back at the station."

"It's probably shite on purpose, to act as a deterrent, preventing us from taking too many coffee breaks."

Bob laughed. "You've got that right."

A man appeared behind the bar and spoke to the barmaid. She pointed in their direction, and he nodded and walked towards them.

"Hi, I'm Matt. Cheryl told me why you're here. If you want to come through, I'll line the disc up ready for you to take a look."

"That's great. Can we bring our drinks with us?"

"Please do."

They followed Matt behind the bar and into a small room at the rear of the dingy hallway. "One day I'll get around to decorating out here. You know what it's like, all work and no extra time to take care of the necessities in life."

"I hear you," Sam said. "Have you had this place long?"

"Nearly ten years. It's okay, we're just scraping by after the pandemic, glad things are now back to normal, or there-abouts. I suppose I should have got my finger out and deco-rated during lockdown. The honest answer is, I was too stressed out wondering how I was going to pay the bills, I didn't really have the funds to sink into making this place pretty, out here anyway. I gave the bar area a quick lick of paint, which the punters appeared to appreciate when we opened the doors again."

"We're still living through tough times, glad you've remained open. A lot of pubs have closed their doors, never to reopen."

"I know, I count myself lucky every day. Here we go. This is Brian, and this is the other guy that Cheryl was on about."

He pressed Play on the disc.

"Cheryl's description was very accurate, considering she only saw him for the first time a few days ago," Sam said.

"She's got a very keen eye, that one. Can spot trouble a mile off before it erupts. Saved my bacon a few times over the years with her intuition."

"Are you on duty in the bar much?" Sam asked, her gaze still glued to the screen, watching the friendly interaction going on between Brian and this stranger called Ian.

"Most nights, but I generally take Mondays off."

"Have you seen this man before?"

He peered at the screen and then looked up at Sam. "Can't say I have, no. I wouldn't class him as local either, dressed like that. Most of our punters wear casual clothes, jeans or sweat pants mostly."

"So he would stick out if you saw him." Sam's gaze was drawn back to the man. He was definitely the bloke who had taken Brian back to his boat that night, the one she had viewed on the other footage she'd obtained from Elsie.

"Do you need a copy of this?"

"If you would."

"No problem. I can do it now for you."

"How well did you know Brian?" Sam asked.

He inserted a new disc and set the machine in motion, then answered, "I suppose he's been coming in here on and off for the past five or six years. Always found him pleasant enough to chat to. Fond of his drink like most fellas are these days."

"What about girlfriends? Was he one for the ladies?"

Pausing to think, he ejected the disc and placed it in the plastic case which he handed to Bob who was the nearest to him. "I suppose he's brought a few girls in here a couple of times."

"Anyone recently?"

"Now you're asking. No, I don't think so. The last one must be over a year ago. Mind you, he's usually in the pub alone, so he's not likely to meet girls that way, is he? Not nowadays, what with all the dating sites around."

"Fair point. Okay, if there's nothing else you can share with us, we'll leave you to it."

"Sorry I couldn't give you anything else. I hope you find the person responsible. I don't think he was the type to get into bother with folks, not from what I could tell."

They retraced their steps through to the bar.

47

"We appreciate your help anyway," Sam said. "All right if we have another chat with Cheryl before we leave?"

"Of course. I can take over from her, not that we're that busy."

Cheryl came towards them. "Is there something else I can help you with?"

"We're going to need to get a statement from you."

"What, now?"

"No, would it be all right if I sent a uniformed officer round to see you when you're not on duty?"

"That would be better. What if I give you my mobile number?"

"Perfect. I can get the duty sergeant to call you to make the arrangements."

"I've never had to make a statement before, is it something I should be worried about?"

"Not at all. The officer will just take down your account of what you saw and heard on Monday evening. There's really nothing to it."

"Phew, okay."

She fired off her number, and Bob jotted it down.

"Thanks for all your help," Sam said before they left the bar.

Outside, she looked up and down the street.

"What are you thinking?" Bob asked.

"I've lost my bearings. Which way is it back to the harbour?"

"Likewise. Let me check." He withdrew his phone and brought up the map. "We're here, let me shrink the map. Ah yes, we're here and the harbour comes into view here."

"So which way would we go? Down the road or up?"

"Down, we're a few streets away from the harbour."

"How long would it take to stagger there?"

"How long's a dinosaur poo? That would be a better question."

Sam wrinkled her nose. "Why do you always have to lower the tone?"

"I'd hate to disappoint you, it's what you've come to expect from me, isn't it?"

"I'm trying to be serious. How long?"

"I would say around fifteen minutes, maximum. What are you thinking?"

"I'm not sure. I suppose I was wondering if they might have stopped off elsewhere after leaving here. We've got them both on two cameras now, that should be enough."

"We might be able to get an adequate still off the discs. We can start circulating his photo, maybe use the media to help identify him."

"I was thinking along the same lines. We'll see. Let's get back, see how the boat-to-boat enquiries are doing."

"Funny. I see what you did there."

Sam rolled her eyes. "I haven't totally lost my sense of humour, you know."

"Haven't you?" Bob said and quickly took a step back to avoid getting a clout from her.

They arrived back at the harbour to find yet more rubberneckers in the crowd.

"What is this fascination about death with these guys?" Sam asked.

"Beats me. I wouldn't hang around, given the choice."

"Ditto. I have far too much to do." She approached a couple of uniformed officers. "Anything to report?"

The younger of the two men opened his notebook and ran his finger down the page. "Nothing of importance, ma'am."

"Hard to believe, isn't it? A man is tortured and murdered,

and not one person either heard or saw anything out of the ordinary."

"Looks that way. Do you want us to broaden the enquiries to the shops now?"

"Yes, do that, not that it's going to be much use plus I've already been to a few. We've got footage of the assailant arriving and we know he used gaffer tape to silence the victim, so I wouldn't waste too much time on it. Did any of the neighbours know Brian well?"

"The guy in the boat on the opposite side of the jetty said they went out occasionally for the odd beer."

Sam's gaze drifted down the jetty to the boat in question. "What's the man's name, do you know?"

The officer flicked through his notebook. "Ah, here it is. Nigel Williams."

"Ah, okay. We've established that he was drinking on Monday evening with a bloke called Ian. Have you come across anyone with that name?"

The two officers looked at each other and shook their heads. "Sorry, no."

Des joined them. "Right, we're ready to move the body now. I don't suppose you've had any joy, have you?"

"Sort of. We've got footage of the victim coming home with someone who we're presuming was a friend. He left a little while later before a person dressed all in black arrived."

"The killer? Was he stalking the place? Or the victim? Watching his movements and then he pounced once he was alone?"

"Potentially, yes. The investigation has started in earnest, all we've done is carried out the preliminary checks. We're just heading back to the station to analyse the footage more."

"Good, let me know if you want the lab to take a look at what you have."

"I will. When will you be performing the PM?"

"Possibly later today. I've got one already booked in for early afternoon, that has to take priority as the family are keen to bury him."

Sam frowned. "Any reason why?"

"I didn't ask. What? You think that's an unusual request? It's not, I get it all the time. I put it down to the way some people deal with their grief. Anyway, that's where we are at with this one. I haven't found anything out of the ordinary on the boat."

"Keep in touch." Sam stepped back, allowing a couple of SOCO techs past with their equipment.

"You do the same, if you would."

CHAPTER 3

"Tell me again, you know, what you did."

He was getting a little tired of recapping the gory details but he was desperate to see her face light up one more time. She'd been in the doldrums for months. This was the first sign of her returning back to normal after…

"This is the last time. I'm bored of hearing my own voice."

She held his hand in both of hers. "I'm sorry, it just means so much to me. To know that he suffered. It's just a shame he was too drunk to realise what was going on and that his life was about to end."

"Oh, believe me, that didn't matter. I could see the fear and realisation dawning in his eyes with every stab. The fucker suffered, my love, no fear of that. Just like the others will."

Miranda tipped her head back and laughed until the tears ran down her cheeks. "Music to my ears. They deserve to suffer after what they put me through. You're my guardian angel for looking out for me like this."

"I hate to see you being tormented by these memories, sis.

It's my pleasure to get rid of these fuckers before they turn their charms on another woman and treat her the same."

She placed a hand on his cheek, and he leaned into it. "You're such a wonderful person. Why a woman hasn't snapped you up by now is totally beyond me."

He knew, however, he had no intention of telling her. She was oblivious to what had gone on in his life over the years since he'd moved away from the family home. It was a secret he intended to keep until his dying days.

He offered up a smile to deflect her concern. "Their loss, sis. Don't worry about me. How are you feeling now?"

"I'm on the top of the world compared to when you first came back home. And that's all down to you and the plans you've put together. It may sound like I'm overstating things here, but you've literally given me my life back. I can never thank you enough for that, Tim. You've been my saviour and will continue to be in the coming days, weeks, however long it will take." She swept her long, curly, mousy-brown hair over one shoulder. It was a motion she'd performed every day of her life since she had spotted their mother, God rest her soul, doing it when she was old enough to realise the effect it had on men.

"You're beautiful, just like our mother. You two were always like peas in a pod. I loved her dearly but I love you even more. You're perfect, and it tears me apart knowing what these men did to you. Why? Why did you allow them to treat you like that?"

She sniffled and shrugged. He could see that he had set her off again with his daft words.

"Don't. I don't want to spoil the euphoria I'm feeling right now. I can't bear to think of the pain and torment they put me through."

"Then don't look back. We'll sort this. Promise me that you will continue to move forward."

Miranda's gaze dropped to the marks on her wrist. He cringed at the thought of her attacking her own flesh with a knife or a razor blade, she'd never confirmed which she'd used. Knowing that she had attempted to take her life had tipped him over the edge. He hadn't hesitated in coming home to be with her, to watch over her. Lord knew she needed someone to do that after the shitty details had emerged of how the men in her life had treated her. He was determined to redress the balance, once and for all.

His plans hadn't taken long to form. He'd penned his intentions and shown them to Miranda. At first, she had whacked him around the face, completely horrified by his suggestions. But all that had changed the second she woke up and came down the stairs for breakfast the following morning. She seemed far brighter, the gloominess had evaporated, and a new vigour for life had emerged. Her smile had reappeared, and it had reminded him of their childhood, the days when she had always been fun-loving and giggling about silly little things. Treasured moments in their chequered past.

He had given up his life to come back to be her saviour. It had been worth it to see the change in her over the months. He had always worshipped her, along with his mother. His father was a different story entirely. Throughout his childhood, he got the impression that he rubbed his father up the wrong way just by breathing most days. He'd been the first to put out the flags the day his father had met his Maker. Tim had spent most of his younger days avoiding being left alone in the same room as him. One wrong look and his father's fists flew in his direction. His sister hadn't really been aware of what he'd gone through over the years. It wasn't until Tim had said that he hated him at the graveside, during the funeral, that Miranda challenged him.

Once the truth had emerged, Miranda had confided in her brother that their father had sexually abused her a few times when she was younger. He hated his father even more, hearing that confession, if that were possible. He had slipped out of the house that night to visit the graveyard where he'd proceeded to piss on his father's grave. Hatred had filled his every pore for days until Miranda had enforced upon him the need to let things go, as far as their father was concerned.

Now it was his turn to repay the favour and to help his sister sort out her feelings once and for all. He couldn't lose her, she was the only family he had left. Their mother had walked out on them years ago, never to be seen again. He'd always had a sneaky suspicion there was more to her disappearance than they had been told over the years. He learnt early on in his life that what his father said went, and if anyone dared to challenge him, they tended to suffer the consequences. Deep down, he had a feeling his father had done the deed and killed his mother; there had been something different about him in the days leading up to their mother's disappearance and for a few days after.

His father had put his foot down, instantly ordered them never to mention their mother again. It wasn't until years later that Tim had sat back to assess what might have happened to their mother. Of course, he had never voiced his concerns out loud to his sister because he had no proof. One of his biggest regrets was that he hadn't forced the confession out of their father on his deathbed. It was the not knowing that was gnawing at his insides. Although, since he'd received the call from the hospital about his sister trying to take her own life a few months ago, his priorities now lay with Miranda and getting her better again.

Turning himself into a killer was the first rung of that long ladder. He recognised the next couple of weeks were going to put him under a lot of strain, but the outcome, seeing his sister hopefully smiling and looking forward to the future again, would be worth the trouble.

"Come on, what are you waiting for? Tell me how you fooled him into friending you again."

He hugged her. "You've heard it ten times over already, love. I'm tired, I need to get some rest. It's getting late now."

"I'm buzzing. I've never felt more alive than I do right now. Who knew bumping someone off could give you such a buzz?"

He wished he felt the same way; he didn't, but he wasn't about to let his sister know. No, he would plough on with the mission, all in the name of making her feel better. To see the joy etched into her face.

Tim switched the news on. "Let's watch some TV, I'm all talked out now. I just want to finish off my can of beer and chill for a few minutes then go to bed. I wonder if there will be anything about Coltman on the news."

Miranda sat forward, her elbows digging into her knees, supporting her head on her hands. "Oh, yes, damn, why didn't I think about that? How satisfying it's going to be to hear that his body has been found. It should have been by now, it's two days since you killed him."

He winced behind her, grateful that she hadn't been looking at him. He hated her speaking about death in such a blasé way. It had taken a lot of courage for him to have set out to befriend Brian, to then take his life.

They sat in silence and listened to the bulletin. There was nothing, no mention at all of the body being found on the boat.

Miranda shot out of her chair and pointed at him. "Are you sure you did the deed? You're not telling me porkies, are you?"

"No, definitely not. I did it. Wait, you saw the blood I had to clean off my clothes and the equipment when I got back."

She glared at him and paced the floor. "You could have killed a feral cat for all I know."

"I didn't," he growled, pissed off by her suggestion and apparent lack of trust. "I can't believe that you think I would deceive you like that."

"You know I don't trust men. Every single one of them has let me down over the years. What's to say you're not about to do the same?"

"Bloody charming. I put my life on the line for you, killing the no-good fucker, or one of them, who ruined your life, and this is the damn thanks I get for it."

She threw herself back on the sofa beside him and collapsed against his chest. "I'm sorry. My head's a mess right now. I didn't mean to accuse you of lying. I know you only have my best interests at heart. Please forgive me."

He flung an arm around her. "There's nothing to forgive. Let's move on. We have others we need to punish, unless you want to call it a day?"

She sat upright and stared at him. "No way. I want them all to die."

"Then we should plan out our next attack."

The smile reappeared and sat comfortably on her thin ruby lips.

CHAPTER 4

*T*he next couple of days were full-on for Sam and her team. She arrived at work on the Friday morning feeling positive that the information they had gathered so far would achieve the results needed to arrest the killer.

"Good morning, everyone. How is the walking wounded today, Alex?"

His left arm in a sling, he swivelled his chair to face her. "I think my dating days are limited at the moment, boss."

"Hallelujah! That'll be music to the ears of dozens of women over the age of forty in Workington."

"Gee, thanks. I'm not *that* bad."

"Says you. Seriously, if you need to take time off to recover from those dreadful injuries, you only have to ask, you hear me?"

"It's not in me to take time off. It's a few bites and cuts, nothing I can't handle. As long as I can still type with my right hand, I'm good to go."

"You're a trooper. I'm grateful for having you on my team. What's happened about the dog that attacked you?"

"It's awaiting a decision. It was the boys' fault, not the dog's. I think I'm going to speak up for it at the hearing."

"You'd do that?" Sam asked, shocked by the notion.

"On one proviso, yes."

"And what's that?"

"The kids do some form of community service and the dog gets taken away from them."

"Sticky wicket with that one, Alex."

He frowned, as if doubting she was right.

"For a start, the dog has attacked a human. You are human, aren't you?" She grinned at him, and he tutted. "Anyway, that'll go against it in the rehoming stakes. Also, the kids will probably deny they set the dog on you in the first place."

"Yeah, I suppose you're right. I never thought about that. Oh well, I guess I'll keep my mouth shut then. See what the decision is when it's made."

"I would. Once a dog has attacked, it's always likely to do it again in the future. I hope you feel better soon."

"I'm fine. Don't worry about me. I might have to stay on desk duty for a few weeks, though, if that's acceptable with you, boss?"

"Of course it is." She turned her attention to the team. "Right, let's recap where we are. Our main priority is still focussed on finding this Ian. When I finally spoke to Warren Podger, the friend who discovered the victim, he was none the wiser about someone called Ian. He regarded himself as a good friend of Brian's and seemed perplexed that he had been out on the piss with the other man. Which tells me that either Brian met this man on the night of his murder or he'd hooked up with him a few days prior. Either way, we need to find this man and see what he can tell us. I've put off using the media on this one for a few days but I think now it's time to call on them. Let's face it, we're stumped without their input. To recap, we've worked out that Brian and Ian left the pub and didn't stop off anywhere else on the way back to the boat, the time stamps of the videos indicate that."

"I take it the victim's father didn't know about this Ian chap either?" Claire asked.

Sam shook her head. "Nope, he was very distant when Bob and I visited him. He didn't seem upset about his son's death in the slightest. Told us their relationship had been strained for years, since his mother had walked out. Heartless is the word I would use to describe him."

"Yep, heartless bastard pretty much sums him up," Bob agreed.

"Nevertheless, we've all dealt with family fall outs before. I'm not about to put his father in the frame, not when we have the two discs of footage at our disposal. Right, if there's nothing else, I should get on to Jackie Penrose, see if she can line up a press conference to go to air today."

Sam walked into her office and shuddered. It felt cold and damp in there this morning, reflecting the weather outside on a chilly April day. From her window, the snow on the hills in the distance was visible. "Damn climate change. Where are the beautiful spring days we used to cherish when I was a kid?"

"Long gone. I'm surprised you can remember that far back. And before you think about throwing something at me, I've brought you a cup of coffee, you wouldn't want to spill it."

She spun around to see her partner standing there wearing a smug grin. "You can go off people, you know."

"I think you went off me years ago, truth be told. You simply tolerate me nowadays."

She placed a hand over her heart. "I feel mortally wounded by that retort, Bob."

"Yeah, they say the truth hurts." He put the cup on the

edge of her desk and fled the room, leaving her staring after him, open-mouthed.

Bloody cheek! You wait, buster, I'll get my revenge when you're least expecting it.

She hitched off her coat and hung it up on the coatstand in the corner. The wind must have changed direction as the rain was now battering her window. Sam took a seat behind her desk, had a few sips of coffee and dialled Jackie's direct line. She watched a couple of raindrops having a race down the pane of glass to the bottom.

"Hello, Jackie speaking, how can I help?"

"Hey, Jackie, how's it going? Are you busy at the moment?"

"Hi, Sam. It's all hunky-dory around here at present. What do you need? And how urgently do you need it?"

"I have a victim and footage of a man he was with, who I need to identify ASAP. Can you fit me in today?"

"Let me check the schedule." Several pages flicked over at the other end. "Ah yes, I've got one slotted in for eleven. I could have a word with the journalists during that, see if they're willing to come back this afternoon."

"About two would be super for me."

"Okay, consider it done. Any drawbacks and I'll get in touch."

"You're a star. Thanks, Jackie. I'll see you at two then."

"Or five minutes before as usual."

Sam laughed and hung up. She cast her eyes at the brown envelopes held together with a thick elastic band in her in-tray and decided she didn't have it in her to start on the onerous chore until she'd at least finished her first cup of coffee for the morning.

A few sips later, a text from her sister, Crystal, arrived.

Crystal: *Hi, how are you? Have you heard from him?*

Sam: *Nope, but I'm not stressing about it. I'm fine, don't worry about me. How's the wedding gown business?*

Crystal: *Still up and down, mostly up at the moment what with the summer being just around the corner. Do you want to come over for lunch at the weekend?*

Sam: *Can I get back to you later today? Hectic day ahead of me. New murder case has me pulling my hair out, not sure if I might have to work overtime at the weekend.*

Crystal: *That's not on. No wonder...*

Sam: *Go on, finish what you were about to say/type. No wonder my marriage is on the rocks, right?*

Crystal: *Sorry, I didn't mean anything by that. I've got a customer, gotta fly. Call me later.*

Sam: *Okay. Be good.*

She put her phone to one side, finished off her drink and tackled the brown envelopes vying for her immediate attention. She'd just discarded two of the envelopes which consisted of advertising circulars and was about to open the third one when her mobile rang. Des Markham's name lit up the caller ID screen.

"Hi, Des. I sense I'm not going to like this call, am I?"

"Your guess would be accurate to ninety-nine-point-nine percent. I've got another dead body if you're interested. Before you reject the offer, I've tried several other DIs and they're all busy, not that you were my last resort, of course."

"Busy? And we're not? What a bloody cheek."

"One of them told me to ring you, stating that you had a larger team than him."

"Don't tell me, it was DI Baldwin, right?"

"I can neither confirm nor deny. Well, are you up for it? Go on, you know you're dying to hear all about it."

"Let me get a pen and paper. Where are you?"

"Seaton, alongside The Royal Oak. Do you know it?"

"Not personally, but I know a man who probably will. What am I attending?"

"Looks like a murder scene to me."

"That's unusual for you to be so definite at this stage. I take it you're talking about yet another gruesome scene then, yes?"

"You could say that. I'd rather leave it there or I'll spoil the surprise."

"Crap. Thanks for the warning. Bob and I will be with you in less than twenty minutes—that's a rough guesstimate, don't hold me to it."

"I won't. See you soon. Make sure you've got some protective suits in the back of that car of yours, too, my supplies are running low."

"Will do." Sam hung up. She picked up her coat and collected Bob on her way out of the incident room.

Downstairs, they stopped off at the supply room as requested and gathered extra suits.

Bob popped them in the boot of Sam's car. "Where are we going?"

"Another murder scene to attend to and, before you ask, no one else is available, so the onus is on us to take it on."

"Huh? Why does it always fall at our door?"

They hopped in the car.

"Let's not think about this negatively," Sam said. "We should be proud that we're considered the best team capable of dealing with such crimes."

"Bullshit!" he said with a cough.

Sam couldn't help but laugh. "It is what it is, partner. We need to deal with it." She pulled out of the car park and into the traffic.

They arrived at the grassy area close to the pub to find Des deep in thought.

"Everything all right, Des?" Sam called over.

Bob collected a couple of protective suits from the boot and handed her one to step into.

"Oh, hi. Yes, just trying to figure a few things out."

She followed his gaze over to the taxi off to the right, its driver's door open, but she was puzzled to see no one inside the vehicle. "Care to fill us in?" She zipped up her suit and moved towards the car.

"Sorry, yes, I'm back with you. I'll show you now. You can tell me what you make of the scene."

They walked past the cordon.

Sam signed the Crime Scene Log held out by the uniformed officer on duty, strode around the car, and there, lying five or six feet from it, tied to a tow rope, was the body of a man. "Ouch! Oh Christ, was he dragged?"

"Yes, the drag marks go from one end of the park to the other. They started on the road over at the entrance and ended up here."

The three of them stepped closer to the victim. Despite the rain lashing down, the victim was still a bloody mess.

"Can I ask why you haven't erected a tent yet?" Sam asked.

"There's no need to check up on us, Inspector. It's all in hand. One of my team has gone back to the lab after finding the tent we had on board was damaged. A mishap no one could foretell happening."

Sam raised her hands. "Okay, I only asked, no need to snap my head off. I was perturbed it hadn't been done yet. I know how efficient you usually are."

"Why thank you, I'll take that as a compliment. Back to the matter in hand."

"Fair enough. Who found the body?"

"That man sitting in his car over there. He generally comes for a run around the park every day. He's in shock, not making much sense the last time I checked, so I'd take it easy on him when you get around to questioning him."

"Don't worry, I'll be my usual gentle self. Bob, get on the phone to the taxi company, see what you can find out."

Bob withdrew his phone from his pocket and ran back to the car to make the call.

"At least he has the sense to find cover from this blasted rain."

The hood of Sam's suit was already soaked through. "Yeah, maybe I should have thought about that and placed the call myself."

They both laughed.

"Who does a thing like this?" she said. "A punter narked at the cost of the ride? Or someone with a vendetta against the driver?"

"I'm erring on the side of caution and going with the latter. The first scenario wouldn't seem likely to me. Saying that, who can bloody tell these days? People's patience appears to be at an all-time low, doesn't it?"

"Sign of the times, I agree. We're getting more and more murder cases to solve lately."

"Go on, say it… since the pandemic struck."

"It's true. Admittedly, there was a lull during the lock-down period, but when some sort of normality returned, the figure we were dealing with this time last year has doubled, or is that my imagination?"

"Judging by how busy my mortuary is, I'd say you were spot on with your assumption. Anyway, that's not going to help this chap."

"Any ID on him?"

"In the car. We've got his identification hung up on the rear-view mirror. Ed Abbott."

Bob rejoined them. "That's right. He got the call around

midnight last night to pick up a woman. Control didn't hear from him after that."

"I take it they didn't chase him up?" Sam asked her partner.

"Nope. Very slack in my opinion. They presumed he went straight home after the fare."

"What a way to run a business. What's the point in being in contact with your staff via radio if you can't be bothered to get in touch with them? Ignore me, it was a rhetorical question. Did you get his address, Bob?"

"No. They wouldn't give it to me over the phone, told me to drop by the office, want us to produce our IDs before they hand over the information."

"Oh right, it's not beyond them to do something right then. Okay, let's see what Des has to tell us and then we'll shoot over there. A woman? Can you see a woman doing this?"

Bob and Des both shrugged. "Maybe she had an accomplice," Bob replied.

"Could she have led him into a trap?" Des suggested.

"Seems the most likely option. The question we need answering is, why? Was he targeted for being him or possibly targeted because he was a cabbie?"

"Does it matter?" Des asked. "The outcome is the same. He perished in the brutal attack."

"Of course it matters," Sam corrected him. "It comes down to motive; we need to know what we're dealing with. Would he have died instantly?"

Des tapped a gloved finger against his cheek. "The likelihood is no, however, it depends. I won't be able to give you an exact COD until I've opened him up. It's possible his heart gave out not long after he was tied up, you know, before the dragging began. If it didn't, we would need to know the speed at which the vehicle was travelling in order to establish how long the torture lasted. That's my take on it. There are too many variables to know for certain at this stage."

"The pick-up was around midnight, you said, Bob?" Sam asked, her mind gathering momentum like a tornado.

"That's right. I suppose we can get a definitive answer when we show up at the cab office. They were a bit too evasive for my liking."

Sam raised an eyebrow. "Sounds fishy. I wonder why. Okay, what else do we have, Des? Any other injuries from what you can tell, not associated with him being dragged, or am I talking out of my arse as usual?"

Des grinned. "I'd agree with the latter. The problem is, we don't know how fast the vehicle was travelling. It might have been that intense that he twisted constantly, therefore, it would give us a false assessment. He may have been battered over the head first, knocked unconscious, allowing the perpetrator to tie him up, or he might have had a gun held to his head by an accomplice while the rope was attached. All this is conjecture at the moment."

"Okay, I understand. Either way, he died a terrible death. If there's nothing else you can add, we'll be on our way then."

"Umm… are you forgetting about the witness?" Bob reminded her.

Unfortunately, she had. The need to get out of the atrocious wind and rain had fogged her brain. "Ugh… okay, let's get this over with."

Sam and Bob walked towards the witness's vehicle. He lowered the window as they approached.

She produced her ID. "Can we jump in the back?"

"Sure. Okay."

They ripped off their suits and left them in an evidence bag beside the car. Once they were inside, the man twisted in his seat to speak with them.

"It was such a shock finding him like that. I've never come across anything like this before."

"I'm sorry you were subjected to it," Sam said. "What time did you find him?"

"I arrived later than normal today—it's my day off work, I delayed coming out early because of the weather. When it looked like it was in for the rest of the day, I thought sod it and came out anyway. I suppose I got here at around nine or thereabouts."

Bob had his pen and notebook poised.

"Did you notice anyone else hanging around?" Sam asked.

"No. There was no one but me here. The thing is, I couldn't make out what I was seeing to begin with, you know, as I drove in. Whether it was because the rain was obscuring my view, I don't know. It wasn't until I brought the car to a halt and peered hard that I could make out what I was seeing. I wish I had shied off coming out today, but if I'd done that, I dread to think who might have discovered his body, probably a bunch of kids or some-thing. In a way, I'm glad it was me. Can you imagine how someone else might feel? Sorry, I'm prattling on, I think it's the shock."

"Don't worry. It can't be easy."

"I suppose you get used to seeing dead bodies daily in your job. This is my first time. I almost threw up when I went over there. I know I should have kept my distance but I needed to see if he was still alive and what type of help, if any, he needed. I did a first-aid course at work. Lot of good that was in his case."

"Did you touch the body?"

"I felt for a pulse on his neck. Did I do the wrong thing? I guess I did. I'm sorry. I was torn by whether I should help him or not."

"No, you did what came naturally. We'll need to take a

DNA and fingerprint sample from you before you leave, just to eliminate you from our enquiries."

He ran a hand through his hair. "I shouldn't have touched him. You have to believe me, I had nothing to do with this. Please, you can't put me on the suspect list."

Sam touched his arm. "Calm down. I assure you, you're not a suspect. It's just procedure, I promise. It's for your benefit. Are you all right?"

His tongue ran over his top lip and then the bottom. "The honest answer is, I don't know. Finding him and then having to wait around has set my nerves on edge. Is that normal? Does it make me look guilty? Because I've never done anything wrong in my life, nothing illegal, I mean."

"Honestly, it's a natural response. You have nothing to worry about as far as we're concerned. If anything, we're extremely grateful for you reporting the incident. Please try to calm down. I know that may be easier said than done, but if you don't, you'll end up making yourself ill."

"I'll try. Can I go now? I've been sitting here for over an hour, getting cold, and I could do with a hot drink to warm me up. Again, it might be the shock making me tremble and feel so cold."

"Bob, can you ask a tech to take Mr... Sorry, I didn't get your name."

"It's Phil Davidson."

"... Mr Davidson's DNA? And then we can let him get on with his day."

Bob shot out of the car.

"All right if I call you Phil?"

"Yes, that's fine."

"We're going to need to take a statement from you in the next day or so, will that be okay?"

"I can't tell you anything else other than I've already told you."

69

"I know. We just need to get things written down. I'll get a uniformed officer to visit you. Would later today be suitable for you?"

"Yes, the sooner we can get it out of the way the better as far as I'm concerned."

"I totally understand. I'm going to need your address in that case."

She jotted down his address in her notebook. Seconds later, Bob returned with the technician, and he took a buccal swab from the man.

"Can I go now?" Phil asked anxiously.

"Yes, you're all clear now. I'll get the station to give you a call later to make arrangements."

"Okay." He started his engine.

Sam said farewell and exited the car. Phil put his foot down, and the tyres skidded a little until he took his foot off the accelerator. He threw Sam an apologetic smile.

"Poor sod. He was really shaken up," Sam stated.

"I'm sure I'd be the same if I wasn't in this job. Where to now? The taxi firm?"

"Yes, we'll need to obtain the victim's address before we can contemplate getting in touch with any next of kin."

Sam went back to Des. "We're going now. The witness couldn't really tell us much. He didn't see anyone else around when he arrived."

"That's a shame. Was he okay?" Des asked.

"In shock and eager to get home."

Des nodded. "He'll be all right after he gets a stiff drink inside him."

"We're going to call in at the taxi office now, unless you have anything else for us?"

"Nope, we'll carry out the usual here. I'll be in touch later after I've performed the PM."

"Look forward to hearing the results. Speak soon."

CHAPTER 5

 $\mathcal{W}$ orkington Taxis' office was on the edge of town. Sam remembered the shop being a chippie when she was younger.

"Seems to be a lot of cabs here," Sam noted. There were taxis parked on the pavement on either side of the road.

"I bet the residents get pissed off if this is a regular occurrence."

"Can't argue with that statement. Let's see what they have to say."

As she opened the door, Sam was confronted by angry men shouting at each other. There was a short man in the middle who was gesticulating with his hands. At the same time he was ordering the men to calm down.

Sam cleared her throat. "Morning, gents. Do you want to keep the noise down a touch, you know, to be respectful to the neighbours?"

"Sod them," a bloke with a straggly beard and matching haircut said. "We've lost one of our own, we're entitled to be upset."

"I'm not saying you're not, let's just keep the noise down

and have a little respect all the same," Sam insisted. She flashed her ID. "DI Sam Cobbs, and this is my partner, DS Bob Jones. Who's in charge around here?"

"That'll be me. Dave Penny," the guy in the middle said.

"Is this normal? To have this many of you in the office at the same time?"

"No. The men are worried. They've come to voice their concerns. We're trying to figure out what to do for the best."

"Sorry, in what respect?" Sam asked, a tad confused.

"Hark at her. What's she on, for fuck's sake?" a tall man at the rear shouted.

"Oi, back off, mate. She's only trying to do her job. Instead of mouthing off, why don't you tell us what's bothering you?" Bob reprimanded him.

"In case you hadn't noticed, one of our associates got killed last night. You're acting like we should get on with our work and not give two hoots about it," another man at the front shouted.

Bob shrugged. "Are we? You haven't given us a bloody chance to say anything yet. Why don't we all cool down and talk about this in a reasonable manner?"

Sam felt a sense of pride, standing alongside her partner. "He's right. Give us a chance."

"I wouldn't mind," Dave interjected, "but this is the second driver we've lost in the past three years. Both murdered, both while on duty. You can understand the men feeling restless and angry about this."

Sam and Bob shared a puzzled glance.

"Two murders? How did the other one die?" Sam asked.

"He had his throat slit by a druggie, apparently. They caught the bastard a few weeks later. We thought we'd got over that incident, and now this. How did Ed die?" Now that the room appeared calmer, Dave went back to his seat at his desk.

"I'm only divulging the nature of Ed's death because I believe you have a right to know."

"Get on with it," came a shout from the back of the room.

Sam glared at the one who had shouted. "Unfortunately, it would appear that Ed was dragged to his death."

"What? How?" Dave asked, jumping to his feet again.

"We believe someone tied a rope to his legs and attached it to his cab then dragged him across a park."

The drivers all stared at each other. Some tutted and shook their heads.

"Jesus," Dave eventually said. "Why? Do you know?"

"No, we've only just started our investigation. We're hoping someone here might be able to help us out with a possible motive."

Dave shook his head and fell into his seat once more. "I can't believe we're here today discussing this. You think we should know why this happened to him? You're wrong. All my drivers are above board, unlike other firms in the area."

A notion flew through Sam's mind. "Have you had a recent falling out with a competitor?"

"Nope. We're the best firm in the area, we play things by the book, no underhand stuff, no undercutting anyone's prices. There's no need. What about that bitch who he picked up last thing? Have you had a word with her yet?"

"Hardly, this is our first stop. We'll need the fare's name and address. We'll also need Ed's next of kin before we leave. Was he married?"

"No. He was living with his girlfriend. I'll get the details for you. As for the fare, she called for a taxi to pick her up in town and said she wanted dropping off at her fella's place, close to The Royal Oak pub. That's where he was found, wasn't it?"

"He was," Sam confirmed.

"Sonya will be in pieces when she finds out. She kept

ringing the night controller all night, demanding to know where he was," one of the younger blokes at the front of the crowd said.

"And where did she believe he was?" Sam asked.

"We told her he must have fallen asleep somewhere or something like that. She didn't believe us. She accused us of lying for him and said when she got her hands on him, he'd be sorry."

"Were there trust issues in the relationship?"

The man nodded. "He rarely kept his dick in his trousers. A few of us warned him he'd get found out eventually."

"Okay, we're going to need more from you than that," Sam stated, her mind racing. Maybe we're dealing with a jealous boyfriend here? If he's guilty of dipping his wick where it wasn't wanted, we could be looking for a boyfriend or husband after revenge.

"Trouble is, I don't want to get involved," the same chap said.

Sam frowned. Confused, she asked, "May I ask why?"

"If his philandering ways have led to his death… well, why would any of us want to get involved?"

She sighed. "If everyone felt like that about an investigation, we'd never get any cases solved. We need your help. Please, won't you reconsider?"

Murmuring and shuffling broke out in the crowd.

"Well, if you put it like that, I can have a gander through the records and see what I can find for you. There are at least three regulars he's knocked off in the last six months."

Dave stepped forward and held out a slip of paper for Sam. "That's bloody news to me," he grumbled. "Here's Sonya and Ed's address. Go easy on her. I'm warning you, she's a sensitive soul."

"In what way?" Sam asked, intrigued by the declaration.

Dave tapped the side of his head. "She has mental problems."

"Sorry? In what context?"

"What the boss is trying to say is that she has mental health problems, along with around eighty percent of the UK population after the bloody lockdown," one of the drivers said.

"All right, Jack, I can speak for myself. I don't need you butting in on my conversations," Dave retaliated with a glare.

"Only trying to help, boss. I'll keep my mouth shut in the future."

"That'll be the day," another driver roared from the rear.

"Whatever. Screw you, arsehole."

"Gentlemen, language, there's a lady in the room," Dave warned.

Sam laughed. "Don't mind me, I hear worse down at the station. If I give you my email address, will you send me the names of the women as soon as you can?" she asked the man who had suggested looking through the records.

He nodded, and she handed him a card.

"Okay, gents, if there's nothing else you can tell us, we're going to leave you to it, go visit Sonya to break the news. I take it no one has rung her since hearing about Ed?"

"We debated long and hard about doing it but decided the news would be better received if it came from the police," Dave admitted.

"Fair enough. Thanks for your help."

"Hey, before you go, what about offering us drivers some form of protection then? Two drivers bumped off and you're just going to walk away and do nothing about it," the tall man at the back shouted.

"I'll get one of my team to take the two cases into consideration, but with the perpetrator behind bars for the first murder, I think it's unlikely there is a connection."

"In other words, you think the two deaths are a coincidence and unrelated?" the tall man queried.

"I'll look into it, but yes, I'm putting my neck on the line and telling you that I don't believe they're connected." Sam smiled and reached into her pocket to extract a handful of business cards. "I'll leave these here if anyone wants to get in touch with me, you know, if you either hear anything or if something suddenly springs to mind that you think I should know about."

She and Bob left the office and headed back to the car.

Bob heaved out a sigh once they were seated. "I thought there was going to be trouble for a moment or two back there."

"I did, too, initially. I don't suppose we can blame them being antsy if they think there might be a pattern."

ED AND SONYA'S house was a mid-terrace on what appeared to be a cluttered street. Cars dotted the roads and the pavements, along with plenty of kids' toys and bikes.

"What a mess," Sam noted as they got out of the car.

"Not the best part of town, is it? The crime rate around here is treble that of other areas in the county."

"And you didn't think to mention that before we arrived?"

Bob shrugged. "I thought you knew this place had a reputation. Sorry."

"Let's get inside and pray the car is still intact when we come out. I'm quite attached to it and haven't got the time to take her to the garage."

"She'll be fine. Make sure you don't disable the alarm, like you usually do."

"Great idea. If she takes us to a room at the front you have my permission to stand by the window, to keep an eye open, while you make notes."

"Want me to stick a trumpet up my arse and play you a tune at the same time, boss?"

"There's no need for you to be sarcastic, partner."

He raised an eyebrow and said, "Isn't there?"

She decided to ignore him and knocked on the front door. It was wrenched open by a young woman who scowled at each of them.

"Yeah, what do you want?"

Holding up her warrant card, Sam announced who they were. "Can we come in and speak to you?"

"About?" Sonya stepped forward and peered left and right up the street.

"It would be better if we spoke inside," Sam insisted.

Sonya humphed, slammed the door against the wall and tore ahead of them up the hallway to a room at the back of the house.

"Jesus, nice welcome. I'm sensing we're in for a tough ride with this one," Bob whispered behind her.

"Let's keep it light and informal and see how we go. She's obviously upset, which is only going to get a lot worse when she hears what we have to tell her."

Sam followed the woman down the hallway and into the kitchen.

Sonya was sitting in a chair at the kitchen table with her back to them, smoking an e-cigarette. "Are you going to tell me what this is all about now?"

"Would it be all right if we sit down with you?"

"Do what you want, just get on with it. In case you hadn't noticed, I'm not in the best of moods because my frigging fella has run out on me. Not a dickybird from him, no call, nothing since last night."

We're in the same boat, except I know your fella isn't going to walk through the door anytime soon. "Okay, I'm not going to beat around the bush. We're here to tell you that Ed was..."

"What? Arrested? No, what for?"

Sam shook her head, thought about reaching out a comforting hand to the sharp-tongued woman but swiftly decided against it. "Sorry, I fear this is going to come as a shock to you. I'm afraid Ed was murdered last night."

Sonya's head jutted forward, and her eyes widened in a horrified stare. After a few numb moments she finally found her voice. "What? This can't be right. Are you sure it was him?"

"Yes. I'm sorry."

She sucked on her e-cigarette and let out two large puffs of smoke. Sam despised the things and waved the billowing cloud away from her face.

"I'm sorry," Sonya said. "I hate these things, but they've kept me calm overnight. I've been ringing the cab company every hour, on the hour. Oh God, did they know he was dead?"

"No, not really, not until his body was found this morning around nineish."

"I'd rip Dave's damn balls off and shove them down his throat if he bloody knew and didn't tell me."

"We asked him not to call you, it's our duty to inform the next of kin or significant other." Sam felt the necessity to tell the white lie to keep the peace between Sonya and Ed's boss.

"How? How did he die? Wait just a second, you said he was murdered, didn't you? I didn't pick up on that before. How? Oh God, why would anyone murder him? For the money? Not that he earnt much, taxi driving is a dead-end job nowadays." She winced as the words tumbled out of her mouth. "I can't believe I said that."

"It's forgotten. We're still awaiting the report from the pathologist but from what we saw of the crime scene it would appear that Ed was dragged behind his taxi. How far and how long is still unknown to us."

"He what? Why? Who would do such a thing? Do you get many deaths like this?"

"I have to tell you this is the first one of this nature I've come across in this area."

"Why him? I know I keep asking the same question over and over, but why? It's not like he fell out with a lot of people, not really. He's had the odd run-in with a tosser or two whilst driving. You know what taxi drivers are like, they make it their mission to cut folks up if they piss them off."

"That's why we're here, as well as breaking the news of his death. We'd like to ask you a few questions, if you don't mind?"

"Anything I can do to help, you only have to ask. It's not right that someone should just go around killing people for no reason."

"In the last few months, has Ed had any form of run-ins with anyone that you can think of? Apart from what you've just told us."

"No, in what respect? Someone not intending to pay their fare, that sort of thing?"

"Possibly. What about a falling out with a neighbour? It seems pretty congested out there at this time of day. I can imagine it can be a darn sight worse come six or seven in the evening."

"Yeah, but everyone has their own space. We live amicably around here despite what outsiders think of the area. It's our home, everyone makes the best of what they've got. We all muck in and help out when the need arises."

"That's good to know. What about finances? By that I mean, could Ed have borrowed some money off someone and not given it back?"

"He might have. If he did, he didn't tell me. He wasn't the sharing type in that respect. What money he earnt he kept for himself. I had a constant battle trying to get dosh out of him to pay for the food he ate. Yes, he covered all the heating bills and other household expenses but he always said the food bills were down to me. He ate out most of the time, so I suppose that was fair enough. It didn't stop him raiding the fridge when he got home at one or two o'clock in the morning, did it?"

"Did he eat at a specific café or restaurant all the time? Or did he mostly grab a burger and eat it in the car on his way to another pick-up?"

"Yeah, that. The taxi always stank of fast food; most of the punters complained about the state of his car. He could be a disgusting pig at times. He said that Dave had recently told him to clean his act up or he'd get booted out."

"And had he?"

"Yeah, sort of. A few weeks ago, he had the car valeted, but when he gave me a ride into town the other day, the car was already beginning to honk again. I dug around under the passenger seat when he filled up with petrol and pulled up dozens of chip wrappings. There are enough bloody bins around this town—typical bloke, he couldn't be arsed most of the time."

Her gaze drifted towards Bob, and Sam had to suppress a grin.

Sam sucked in a breath to prepare herself for the backlash to what she was about to ask next. "And your relationship was solid?"

Sonya glared at her and frowned. "What are you asking? Or are you suggesting that I had something to do with his murder?"

Sam raised her hand. "No, I wasn't suggesting that at all. Your relationship, was it on a firm footing or did you fall out occasionally?"

Sonya rolled her eyes and puffed on her e-cigarette again. "Doesn't everyone? How many people do you know who have a perfect Mills and Boon type relationship? Do you?"

Sam and Bob looked at each other. In the past six months, they had both dealt with problems at home.

"Okay, fair point," Sam said. "I have to ask the question, though: is it possible that Ed may have been carrying on with someone?"

"It's possible, I suppose. I couldn't keep tabs on him day and night. He worked extremely long hours as a driver, at least that's what he told me. Who knows? He could have been giving a woman one behind my back. You know what men are like. Most men I've been out with have cheated on me, it's in their genes, isn't it?"

Sam glanced in her partner's direction again and noticed he had kept his head down this time. *Hmm... is there something you're not telling me, Bob?* "It's a difficult question to answer, I suppose there are a lot of women out there playing around behind their partners' backs as well. I guess it's not gender-specific these days, a sign of the times. Monogamy appears to be a thing of the past."

"For some of us. Don't tar us all with the same brush. I haven't as much as looked at another man since I moved in here with Ed."

"How long had you been together?"

"Around nine months, give or take."

Sam nodded and smiled. "Can you remember how you met?"

"Yep, I was on a night out with the girls, we caught a taxi home. I was the last to be dropped off. I didn't have enough money on me. He thought I was about to do a runner on him, so he followed me into my flat. I had fifty quid stashed under my mattress for emergencies. I asked if he had time for a drink once I'd paid him. He took me up on my offer, and we became an item after that night. Three months later, and I was moving my stuff in here. Not very romantic, but there we go. It suited us both at the time."

"Did he have any family in the area?"

She slapped a hand to her face. "Shit, yes, his mother is due to retire this week. She's going to be horrified when she hears. I'm not expected to tell her, am I? I know I should, but he was her only child, and you know what a mother-and-son relationship is like."

"I do. Do you want us to inform her?"

Sonya blew out a relieved breath. "Would you? That would be great and save me the heartache of reliving the experience over and over."

"We'll need her name and address before we leave."

"I'll get my phone, it's in the lounge." Sonya left the room and returned within a few seconds. Scrolling through the mobile, she managed to locate the details she was after and gave her phone to Bob to note it all down. "She works afternoons at the local library, so you should be able to catch her at home if you're quick."

"Thanks for the tip. What about friends, did he have any close friends?"

"One or two. None that I would call close-close, if you get my drift."

"I do. Okay, I think we'll leave it there unless you have any questions you'd like to ask us?"

"I don't think so. Well, except, what happens now?"

"The pathologist will perform a post-mortem and assess your boyfriend's injuries. After that, we should get a clear indication of how he actually died."

A puzzled expression appeared on her face. "I don't get what you're saying."

"It's possible that Ed might have already been dead before he was dragged."

"Oh, right. Does it matter? He was still murdered, right?"

82

"It's better for us to get a bigger picture of things. Maybe the killer left some DNA on Ed's body, that will be highlighted during the PM as well. Then the pathologist will release the body to the undertaker, might not be for a few days, though, and the undertaker will get in touch with you or his mother, whatever you decide between you, to make the final arrangements for the funeral."

Sonya closed her eyes and opened them again. There were tears swimming in the blue pools. "Will I be able to see him? Is he that bad? Will I even recognise him?"

"I can have a word with the pathologist if that's what you want. Ed will be cleaned up during the PM. Do you think his mother will want to see him as well?"

"Without a doubt. Maybe I should accompany her. That might be more suitable, if we go together. God, the thought of viewing a dead body…"

"Look at it as saying a farewell to someone you loved."

Sonya picked at her fingers. "I'm sat here wondering if I truly loved him. Does that make me sound a bitch?"

"Not in the slightest. Grief can be dealt with in many ways by the victim's family and partners."

"I suppose you're right. All I feel right now is hatred towards him for leaving me in the shit. There, I've said it out loud, shame on me for thinking that way when he's about to be cut up in the mortuary."

Sam covered Sonya's hand with her own. "Don't beat yourself up. I'm sure you'll feel differently about all of this in the next day or two."

"I hope so. I should have asked, do you have any leads at all about who might have killed him? Was it someone he picked up as a fare?"

"We're unsure at present. He did pick up a woman around the time he went missing."

"Missing? What time?"

Sam cringed for opening her big mouth, possibly getting Dave into trouble. "The last time control heard from him was around midnight when he picked up his last fare. He went missing after that."

"Why didn't they tell me?"

"Maybe they were trying to protect you."

"Bollocks. They deliberately hid the truth from me. I want to know why."

Sam sighed. "I'm sorry but I think you have a right to know."

"Know what?" Sonya took a large puff on her vape and stared at Sam.

"The drivers told us that Ed had been known to fool around."

She shrugged and bit the inside of her lip. "Why am I not surprised? I had a feeling he was up to something. All right, I'm going to be honest with you in return. I tackled him about a few things that didn't sit right with me, but he always flat-out denied he was up to something. You know most taxi drivers have flings at one time or another, right? After all, that's how we met, he came on to me after I let him in my flat."

"You told us you made him a drink when you fetched the cash you owed him."

"I know. But one thing led to another, and we ended up..."

"In bed?" Sam filled in, mortified by what the young woman was telling her. Where were young people's morals these days? Get off your soapbox, Sam. The world is a different place to the one I grew up in. Says me, acting as though I'm ancient instead of only being thirty-two.

"No, we didn't get that far, we ended up doing it on the couch in the living room."

"I see. And you started seeing each other regularly after

that?"

"Yes, everything else I told you was true. Once you've found yourself in that situation, I suppose the possibility always lingers in your mind that he will be capable of doing the same with someone else, right?"

"Perhaps. Don't crucify yourself over what direction your mind is going in at the moment. I'm sure we'll find out the reason behind his death, soon."

"I'll try not to. If he was playing away then maybe he got what was coming to him. Sorry, I shouldn't have said that, it was a dumb thing to say."

"Not at all. If that's how you feel. We're going to leave now. Are you sure you're going to be all right? Or do you want me to call someone, ask them to be with you? There's every chance it might hit you hard once we've left."

"No, you go. I'll give my sister a call, fill her in. She's a fusspot, she'll want to come and be with me."

"Good. I really don't think you should be alone at this time, your emotions are clearly in turmoil."

Sonya took another drag on her e-cigarette and nodded. "Hardly surprising after what we've discussed." She stood and showed them to the door.

Sam turned and smiled. "I'll leave you my card. If you need to chat anytime, give me a call."

"Thank you for being so kind. Good luck."

She closed the door behind them.

Sam unlocked the car with her key fob. "See, the car is safer than either of us thought it would be."

Inside, Bob shook his head. "That was a revelation. Do you think she has anything to do with his death?"

Sam faced him and pulled a face. "Do you?"

He shrugged. "The thought had crossed my mind. She did lie to us back there."

"I wouldn't call it that."

"Huh, what would you say it was then?"

"Evading the truth to save face."

Bob groaned. "Whatever, it amounts to the same thing."

"It does not. Right, enough of this, we need to go and break the news to Ed's mother."

"Oh, joy of joys, you definitely know how to show a man a good time."

Sam laughed. "You say the bloody weirdest things. Buckle up, remind me of the address again."

"I like to keep you on your toes, I make it a daily mission." He flicked open his notebook and angled it in her direction.

She punched the road name into her satnav and waited for it to come up with the route. "It's fourteen minutes from here. We'll go break the news and then find a café for some lunch, I'm starving."

"Really, and who's paying?"

"That'll be me then by the sounds of it. You're such a tight-arse with your money, Bob."

"Am I heck? I have bills to pay and a wife and child to support…" His voice trailed off when he realised what he'd said. "Sorry, I didn't mean to rub it in."

"Bloody hell. Do you seriously think I sit here and analyse every single word you say? For your information, I don't. So stop walking on eggshells around me, got that?"

"Hardly, otherwise I wouldn't have opened my big mouth in the first place."

"Whatever," she said.

CHAPTER 6

S am and Bob returned to the station. With Ed's mother now informed and their stomachs full after stopping off at a local café for a sandwich, there was work to do. Bob handed around the sandwiches they had picked up for the rest of the team.

"How are you, Alex?"

"There's no need to keep checking on me, boss, we Scots are made of strong genes. A few nips from a four-legged beast aren't about to prevent me from doing my job."

She patted him on the shoulder without thinking, and he cringed beneath her touch and bit down on his tongue.

"Sorry, I shouldn't have done that. Right, can I have your attention, please?"

The team all turned to face her.

She took a few sips of coffee, picked up the marker pen and proceeded to write another name on the board. "Ed Abbott. Now, I'm not for one minute suggesting the two cases are connected but I have to put his name somewhere. What we're going to need to do is split the team up to cover both cases."

"Remind me again, how many other teams are forced into this position," Bob complained. He folded his arms and sank low into his chair.

"It's something we have to deal with. I know it's not ideal, but there's also no point in us whinging about it either, okay?"

Bob's eyes closed, and he shrugged.

Sam knew it was useless trying to negotiate with him when he was in this mood.

"Okay, where do we stand with the first case?" she said.

"I've been going over the CCTV footage again, from the discs you gave me, and apart from highlighting the two men, I haven't managed to discover anything else, such as reflections in shop windows, any possible vehicles to try and locate," Alex announced. "To me, that signifies that the perpetrator is experienced enough to cover his tracks."

Sam nodded. "Not a chancer in other words."

"That's what I reckon."

"Keep searching, there must be something we can latch on to."

"Aye, I'll do that, boss."

"What about the background checks on Coltman, has anything shown up there, Claire?"

"Nothing. He had enough funds in his bank account to last him for about six months. Very few outgoings in the way of direct debits, as expected since he lived on the boat."

"Any vehicle in his name? I don't recall seeing one at the harbour, do you, Bob?"

His brow creased into a frown, contemplating the question. "Come to think of it, no, I didn't. Would he need one? If he lived on the boat in the centre of town? With so many pubs within walking or, should I say, staggering distance?"

"Fair point. Can you check all the same, Claire? If he had a car and it's gone missing it could lead us to the perp."

"I'll check now, boss."

"Thanks. Right, here's what we know about the second case, feel free to chip in if anything sounds off to you. Ed Abbott picked up a fare from town, a woman passenger who needed to go to near The Royal Oak pub. We have no way of knowing if Abbott tried it on with the woman or whether she led him into a trap, either scenario is a possibility at this stage. The facts as they stand are that Abbott was tied to the rear of his car and dragged to his death. When we showed up at the taxi office, Bob and I were greeted with a bunch of angry drivers, all demanding to know what we were going to do to keep them safe. They made us aware of another death of a driver from a few years ago; there might be a connection, so we need to look into that angle. I think it's a bit of a stretch because the boss of the taxi firm told me the perp was caught and is doing time for the crime. But it's still something we need to delve into, just in case the perp has planned something from the inside."

"Is that likely? Wasn't he a druggie?" Bob interrupted.

"I'd rather do the necessary digging and discount the possibility, partner."

Bob hitched up a shoulder.

"Another thing we learnt from the drivers was that Ed liked the ladies. Although he was living with his girlfriend at the time of his death, he still played around with some of the punters. That could be a direction we need to examine. The boss of the taxi firm is looking into possible punters with whom he had a fling with—hopefully he'll get back to us soon with the information so we can proceed with that angle."

"Is there anything we can do regarding the victim, in the meantime?" Suzanna raised her hand to ask.

"Again, we should inspect the background information. See if there were any likely debts. After we spoke with his girlfriend, she told us the house belonged to him, or she moved in with him. What she didn't tell us was whether the house was mortgaged or rented. Let's see if he had any debts. Apart from that, clues are thin on the ground until Dave gets back to us. With that information to hand we can visit the women concerned and see what they have to say. It's possible that if he treated one of them badly, a boyfriend or husband might have taken the opportunity to dish out some revenge."

"That seems a bit extreme," Bob said.

Sam turned her head first one way and then the other to ease the tension in her neck. "We've heard a lot worse over the years, Bob, you know that. And that, ladies and gentlemen, is all we have right now. I'd like Claire, Liam and Alex to stick with the first case, and Suzanna, Oliver, Bob and I will deal with the second case. Does anyone have any questions at this stage?"

The team all shook their heads.

"Let's get busy then." Sam picked up her cup and walked into her office. A cold breeze brushed over her, so she stopped off at the radiator and turned the thermostat up to five and continued to her desk.

She sat at her desk and inwardly groaned at the mound of brown envelopes that had miraculously appeared overnight. Opening the first one, she set it aside without much hesitation when the phone rang. "DI Sam Cobbs, how can I help?"

"Oh, hello. Yes, umm... we spoke earlier. I'm Sonya Philips. It is you I spoke with, isn't it?"

"Yes, that's right, Sonya. Is there something you need from me?"

"No, not really. Umm... you said if there was anything I thought about after you left, that I should give you a call."

"And is there?"

"Yes. It wasn't until you went that I thought of an incident that happened a few months back, it was around Christmas time, I seem to remember."

"And what was that?" Sam's interest suddenly hit the ceiling and bounced back to her. Pen in hand, she waited for Sonya to respond.

"Well, we woke up one morning, and Ed went off to work. He hadn't been gone long, when he came back into the house, fuming. Cursing and kicking out at the furniture."

"May I ask why?"

"Because someone had keyed the side of his car."

"Ouch, was the damage very bad?"

"Bad enough to warrant a spray job. We were low on funds around the time, so he had to take out a small loan to cover the repair bill. He asked if I could chip in and help out, but money was tight for me back then as well."

"Did that put a strain on your relationship?"

"Yes. He accused me of not backing him, of bleeding him dry. It was all nonsense, of course. I had just forked out for all the Christmas presents, for his family as well as my own, and that's the thanks I got for it. He had the audacity to tell me my priorities were all wrong. I ask you, what is wrong with men? Sorry, I shouldn't be having a go about him, not now he's dead."

"It's okay, it's natural for you to be still upset if the problem caused a rift between you at the time. Did you ever find out who caused the damage to the car?"

"No. He asked all the neighbours, but no one saw anything. It was a mystery."

"Did he have an inkling who was behind it?"

"He had an idea it was a driver from another firm who he had fallen out with around that time. He confronted the bloke on a taxi rank later that week, but the driver denied it and told him he was losing his marbles."

"I bet that went down well."

"Not really. A fight broke out, not a bad one, handbags at twenty paces type of thing. A couple of the other drivers broke it up."

"And what happened afterwards?"

"In what respect?" Sonya asked.

"Did he blame anyone else or did Ed still think the driver was the one who did it?"

"He was adamant it was the driver he confronted. The bloke gave him the evil eye whenever they met after that, which only raised his suspicions even more."

"I see. Can I ask what the cost of the repairs was?"

"Over five hundred quid. Not exactly small change. People think taxi drivers are rolling in it, they aren't. There were days when he made a loss. Have you seen the price of petrol compared to what it was during lockdown? Another fifty pence per litre, and yet it's impossible to put the fares up that much. He had to in the end, but that just meant a significant drop in trade. I'm not blaming the punters, they work hard for their money, too. It's the government and the greedy fat cats in the oil industry that need sorting out. Bastards, they've got everyone by the short and curlies, haven't they?"

Sam sighed. "You're not wrong. The cost of living has escalated for everyone over the last year or so."

"And we all know what that means for you guys. The crime rates are bound to go through the roof, aren't they?"

"Yes, unfortunately, we're definitely seeing proof of that. The crimes are becoming far more serious as well, due to people's frustration often getting the better of them."

"You think this is what's happened with Ed?"

"We're not entirely sure as yet. The investigation is still in its infancy. I'll look into what you've told me, though. Can you give me the name of the driver and what company he works for?"

"Let me think." Sonya paused for a while and then tutted.

"I know it was Gary, no idea what his surname is, sorry. He works for Jack's Cabs in Workington, if that helps."

"I'm sure it will. If there is anything else that comes to mind, will you run it past me?"

"Of course. Can I ask how his mother took the news?"

"I take it she hasn't rung you?"

"No, we weren't what you would call close. I think she tolerated me for Ed's sake."

"Sorry to hear that. She was understandably devastated when I shared the news with her. I had to stay with her for a while to offer some comfort."

"Damn, I feel guilty now. I should have had the courage to come with you."

"No, it's fine. We're used to dealing with people's grief."

"I don't think it's really hit me yet. I can't say I broke down and cried when you left."

"As I say, grief affects different people in various ways. Give yourself a break, you're probably still in shock."

"I'm caught between a rock and a hard place, wondering if I should give his mum a call or not."

"It wouldn't hurt. She might find it hard to comprehend if you don't. Just prepare yourself for her not being in the best frame of mind."

"Thanks for the warning. Okay, I'll leave you to get on with your busy day. Will you keep me informed during the case?"

"Probably not step by step, but if we discover who the killer is, then yes, you'll be one of the first people I get in touch with. Take care, Sonya, and thanks for supplying this information."

"You're welcome. Good luck."

Sam took the details into the incident room. "Bob, can you do me a favour?"

"If I have to," he replied with a churlish grin.

"Ring Jack's Cabs, it's a Workington taxi company, ask if they have a driver called Gary on their books."

He glanced up from his notes. "Is that it? No surname?"

"Nope. You're supposed to ask what happens if they tell you he works for them."

"Oh, am I?" He raised a finger. "Hang on, boss, what do I say next if they confirm they have a Gary working for them?"

She shook her head. "You know what? Words fail me at times. The reason I want to know is because there has been a development."

Bob swivelled in his seat and sat forward, exaggerating his anticipation.

Sam was tempted to clip him around the head but clenched her hand instead. "One of these days, partner... anyway, Sonya has just rung me, told me she recalled an incident that happened around Christmas time. Ed had his car keyed—he suspected this Gary of doing the deed after they fell out around that time. Ed confronted him, but Sonya said that Gary denied it. The bill was paid via a loan which I'm sure will show up in his bank statement."

"Ah, okay, that all makes sense, although it doesn't cover what I asked."

"If you let me finish, I was about to tell you to ask Gary to drop by the station if he's in the area during the day and we'll interview him."

"And what if he runs scared?" Bob asked.

"Then we'll know he's got something to hide, won't we?"

"Will we? Why don't we call round there and tackle him face to face like we usually do?"

Her partner was making a compelling argument, one she didn't have an answer to, for a change. "All right, you win. Grab your coat."

"Wait, if he's a driver, shouldn't I ring the office and see if he's on duty first?"

Sam wagged a finger at him. "Why don't you do as I suggested in the first place and play it by ear, how does that sound?" She turned on her heel. "I'll be in my office, ticking off another item on my to-do list." Then she slammed the door behind her. *The one day I could do without him winding me up he seems to be in top gear.* Back in her seat, Sam decided to check in with Des Markham to ask if there were any updates on the two victims as far as the PMs and other tests were concerned.

"Hi, Des, it's…"

"Don't tell me, yes, it's the girl of my dreams."

Sam's bad mood instantly evaporated into the ether. "You wait until I see Paula next time."

"Gosh, now my knees are knocking. Seriously, have you had a sense of humour transplant in the last few weeks, Detective Cobbs?"

"Tell me this, Doctor, what frame of mind do you think you'd be in if your wife walked out on you and didn't bother to contact you for two weeks?"

"Ouch! Okay, that'll teach me to keep my mouth shut. Sorry, do you want to start this conversation again?"

"It wouldn't be a bad idea, and there's no need for you to apologise, it's my fault for being a grouch. I think my partner would back me up on that, also."

"Oh dear, have you just sunk your teeth into his testicles?" He laughed. "I should say metaphorically speaking, of course."

"You could say that. Sometimes you men just don't know when to call it a day when winding a woman up."

"Oops, he is a naughty boy. Do you want me to have a word with him the next time I see him?"

"Definitely not, I can handle him. Can we get back to business? I have a hectic day ahead of me."

"Agreed, let's try this for a third attempt: what can I do for you, Inspector?"

"I was wondering if you had any news for me regarding either case."

"Nothing on the first case. I've released the body to the coroner. I contacted his father; he wasn't interested in viewing his son's body, just wanted to know what the next step was and how soon we could progress to that stage."

"Blimey, that's a bit harsh. I know they didn't really see eye to eye, but even so we'd need him to view it for the formal identification process."

"Yep, my sentiments exactly, which is why he ended up coming in for that. As for the second victim, I'm just about to open him up. I was delayed at the scene because of the inclement weather—we were forced to take cover a few times when the heavens decided to punish us."

"Sorry to hear that. During your time at the location, did anything else rear its head that I should know about?"

"That's super intuitive of you, Inspector; why yes, something did crop up."

"I'm all ears."

"One of the techs managed to find a few tyre marks in the grass at the other end, away from the body and the car."

"Hmm... do you think it's connected to the crime?"

"I have no way of knowing at this stage. It was tricky because of the downpours we experienced, but we believe we managed to preserve a section of it, just in case."

"That's excellent news."

There was a knock on the door, and Bob poked his head into the room. Sam smiled and beckoned him to join her. He sat opposite while she continued her conversation.

"All right, I'll let you get on then. Will you let me have the two PM reports ASAP?"

"You'll have them tomorrow, without fail. If I find

anything important during the PM this afternoon, I'll give you a call."

"Thanks. Speak soon." Sam suddenly checked her watch. "Damn, I forgot about the press conference." She shot out of her chair as her mobile rang. "Shit! It's Jackie." She answered the call. "Sorry, Jackie. I got held up with something important. I'm on my way now."

"What about the driver?" Bob shouted behind her.

"Tell me when I get back. I'll be half an hour max."

Sam bolted down the stairs, caught her heel on the way down and almost ended up on her arse at the bottom. Jackie was waiting for her outside the conference room, tapping her toe and glancing behind her anxiously.

Sam apologised again. "I couldn't help it. Are they all in there?"

"Yep, ready and waiting. I hope they don't turn on you, you know what these journos are like when they've been held up."

Cringing, she replied, "Actually, I don't, because I've never been late before."

"There's always a first time. My advice would be to apologise and let them know that something unforeseen turned up that you had to attend to urgently."

"I'd be telling the truth," Sam fibbed and avoided eye contact with the press officer.

"We'd better get a wriggle on if you want to escape the next thirty minutes relatively unscathed."

"God, don't say that. I'm nervous enough as it is."

They entered the room and took their seats behind the long table that had been draped with a cloth displaying the constabulary's emblem. The room quietened down, and Jackie introduced Sam and the reason as to why they were there. Then she passed the baton over to Sam, who was grossly unprepared and tried her very best to sound confident, despite her stomach churning like a washing machine on a high spin speed. She asked for any help from the public who may have seen Brian Coltman, and his friend Ian, on the Monday night of that week. She also appealed for Ian to come forward to tell them what he knew about the events of that evening. As a final note, while she had the journalists' attention, Sam made the most of the exposure by mentioning that a second body, unrelated to the first crime, had been found that morning at The Royal Oak at Seaton.

The crowd went quiet until Clive Carter raised his hand. "You're trying to tell us that you have two murders within a few miles of each other in the same week and you're treating them as separate investigations, Inspector Cobbs?"

Sam smiled to combat his aggressive tone. "At present, yes, Mr Carter. As with all our investigations, unless something jumps out at us in the form of *solid* evidence, we'll continue to keep the cases separate."

There were a few more minor questions from a couple of other journalists, and then Jackie brought the conference to a halt.

In the outer room, Sam breathed out a relieved sigh. "Well, that went better than I anticipated, apart from Carter piping up as usual."

"It's what he does best, or worst, depending on your point of view. I hope it helps, it's due to go out on the evening news."

"I'll get someone to man the phones."

"Give me a call if you need anything else, Inspector."

"I will. You're an absolute treasure, Jackie." Sam tore back up the stairs to find Bob sitting at his desk, watching the door for her reappearance. "Right, that seemed to go as planned, or thereabouts. What about the driver?"

"He's on duty now. We'll call in at the taxi office when we need to see him. I said we'd likely be there at around three."

"What? That doesn't give us much time to get out there, does it?"

"It is what it is. He's going off duty at three-thirty; it was either that or we'd catch up with him on Monday as he's busy over the weekend. I thought you'd go for the first option."

"All right. Forget I said anything. Before we head off, I'm in need of a volunteer to man the phones this evening, anyone?"

Liam raised his hand. "I'll do it, boss, with pleasure."

"Bloody creep," Alex mumbled.

Sam shot the older man one of her looks. "Less of the name-calling on my watch, Alex Dougall, you hear me?"

"Sorry, boss."

"Thanks, Liam. It's kind of you to offer. Give it until ten-thirty and then call it a night. If you want to ring for a pizza, I'll stump up for it."

"There's no need. I can pick up a curry on the way home. I'd prefer that, boss, I tend to eat later anyway."

"It's your choice. I'm going to need you to take down the usual. I kept the summary brief, asked if anybody who knew this Ian chap, drinking with Brian on Monday, to get in touch. I added a plea for the man himself to come forward. I also asked the public if anyone had seen anything around midnight at The Royal Oak, at the second crime scene."

"Why? I thought we weren't linking the cases," Bob queried.

"I know. I just thought it was worth mentioning while I had the journos' attention."

Bob scratched the side of his neck. "Okay, I see where you're going. Talking of which, shouldn't we better be making a move? Time's getting on."

Sam glanced up at the clock; it was already two-fifty.

"Yikes, we're going to be cutting it fine. Any idea where the office is?"

"It's all in hand. Five minutes away."

"You could have told me that before, rather than getting me all worked up."

He grinned. "Where would the fun be in that?"

"Anything else before we go, folks?" Sam addressed the rest of the team.

"Just a quick one, boss," Claire called back. "I can confirm Ed Abbott had a loan granted for seven hundred and fifty pounds in early January."

"To cover the repairs plus some by the sounds of it. Great, thanks, Claire. Bob, shall we go?"

"Ready when you are." He slipped his jacket off the back of the chair and hitched it on.

CHAPTER 7

"It's on. Quick, Tim," Miranda shouted. She snuggled under the throw and passed Tim the bowl of popcorn she had made to celebrate the occasion. It's what they had done as kids before the trouble had begun.

"I'm coming." He stood in front of her, holding out a glass of brandy.

She took the drink and waved him out of the way. "You might not care if you miss the bulletin, but I do."

"Of course I care." He threw himself onto the sofa and dug his elbow into her hip.

Miranda lashed out and spilt some of her drink.

"What a waste," he complained.

"Shh… this is it." She upped the volume on the remote control, and they sat in silence.

The inspector mentioned the name Ian, and Tim giggled childishly.

"I told you it would fool them, using a different name," he said. "Nowt clever about the police up here. Thick as cow's muck and twice as smelly."

Miranda put a finger to her lips. "Hush now. I want to hear what she says."

"Why bother? They know fuck all. Correction, they know as much as we've been willing to give them, which doesn't amount to much."

"She seems nice," Miranda noted.

"She's a copper, there's no such thing as a nice copper. Don't go getting soft on me now. We've got work, a lot of work to do, over the coming weeks. I need you to remain focussed at all times."

"Stop nagging. Oops, sorry, it's only women who nag, isn't it?"

He faced her and fixed a smug grin in place. "Yep, you've got it, sis. Like I said, they haven't got much. I noticed she mentioned the two cases but slapped that journalist down when he wondered if the cases were connected."

"You're saying that's a good thing?"

"Yes, we don't want them connecting the cases, not at this stage. I've made sure that shouldn't happen. The fact you were involved in the second crime, I think that was a genius stroke on my part. Looks like the plan worked by putting them off the scent."

Miranda turned the TV down again now that the new bulletin pertaining to them had finished. She took a sip from her drink. "Genius my arse. What are you like? Honestly, you're so full of shit sometimes."

He smiled and emptied his glass. "I'll say one thing."

"What's that?"

"It makes my day to see you so happy. You've been a different person since we said farewell to those two bastards."

"I can't deny it. I feel like the weight of the world has been lifted from my shoulders. I've lived under a constant cloud of shame for years. Men, they have no idea how their actions can turn a woman's life upside down in an instant."

He placed his glass on the floor beside him and gathered her hands in his. "I told you, all that is about to change over the next few weeks. You've lived a life of hell, and the rest of the bastards will pay big time for what they put you through, love."

Miranda twisted in her seat and placed her head on his chest. "I'm so glad I finally broke down and admitted what had been eating me up for years. None of this would be possible if you hadn't come home."

"It's been worth it so far to see the smile return to that beautiful face of yours. For a start, you should never let anyone, male or female, get the upper hand over you. Slap them down when it's needed. You've been a doormat to far too many men over the years. That's going to stop, you hear me?"

"I realise that now. You know me, I'd rather suffer the consequences than deal with confrontation."

"Yeah, and where did it get you? Nowhere, except on the verge of taking your own life."

Miranda's head dipped lower on his chest.

Tim moved slightly and placed a finger under her chin to make her look at him. "All that is forgotten now. Life is for living, and that's exactly what you're going to do. After we get rid of these fuckers once and for all, it'll make you feel complete again, I promise you."

"Then what? Am I likely to find a man like you? Who will worship and respect me? I doubt it."

"Hey, why do you need a man in your life? I haven't got a girlfriend. If it's the loneliness you can't stand, I'll always be here for you, right?"

Miranda forced a smile. "I know. It's not the same,

though, as cuddling up with someone, there's the intimate side of a relationship to consider, too."

"It's not all it's cracked up to be. You've experienced more than your fair share of bad behaviour from men that you could do without. I'll never let you down, sis, ever."

"If you insist."

They cuddled for the next five minutes, each of them deep in thought.

Until Miranda sat upright and announced, "Time is marching on, shouldn't we be getting ready?"

Tim glanced up at the clock on the wall. Ten-thirty. "We should leave in twenty minutes. We'll need to wait in the car until all the customers have gone home before we can attack."

"Okay. I'm going to go upstairs and slip into something more comfortable. I think I've eaten too much popcorn this evening."

They both laughed.

While she ascended the stairs, her thoughts remained on the task ahead of them that evening. It would consist of both of them being involved—she was aware that Peter, their proposed target, would probably put up a fight. It was in his nature. They just needed to be prepared to bring him down before he found his footing to retaliate. They had agreed to wear a disguise for their little adventure. She slipped into her velour leisure suit and sought out her new trainers, buried under her dirty clothes in the corner of the room. *I must get around to doing some washing one of these days. I have so much on my plate at the moment, it's difficult to fit the everyday chores in.* Smirking, she went to the wardrobe and removed a scarlet wig from its plastic cover and positioned it on her head. Shocked at the instant transformation, Miranda nipped to the loo and then descended the stairs.

Her brother took one look at her and released a low whistle.

"How cool is this?" she asked.

"It's amazing. I nearly didn't recognise you. That was a stroke of luck, you spotting that wig advert on the back of the newspaper." He sprang to his feet. "My turn. I won't be a jiffy."

Miranda tidied up the lounge a little, anything to keep her busy as she anxiously awaited his return. *Thud, thud, thud* down the stairs, and then there he was, standing in the doorway.

"Wow, that's simply incredible. I would never guess that was you. The wig is fantastic. You should consider wearing it all the time if it changes your appearance like that."

Tim scratched his head. "You're kidding me! I couldn't wear this itchy thing permanently, it's rougher than a badger's bottom. Still, it won't be for long. What do you think of this?" He patted his rounded stomach, which gave the illusion his frame was two stone heavier.

"Ha, ha, it's brilliant. I didn't even notice."

"You what? What are you trying to tell me?"

She ran into his arms, happier than she had been in years. "What would I do without you to brighten my day?"

"Enough said. Come on, let's get going. We can have a swift one in the pub before we make him pay."

THE FLYING HORSE was relatively quiet when Miranda and Tim arrived.

He parked the car in the corner of the car park to avoid being seen on the cameras. "Are you ready for this? Follow my lead, there's no need for you to be scared. Have you got your glasses? They'll add to your disguise, he shouldn't recognise you then."

"Yes, I've got them in my pocket." Miranda popped them onto the bridge of her nose and fiddled with the sides of her hair in the mirror. "I'm good to go."

"Okay. Nice and cool, all right? Leave the talking to me. You let out an excited giggle now and again, pretending you're enjoying yourself."

"No pretence needed. I'm thrilled to be here." She chuckled.

"Try and contain yourself. Are you ready?" he repeated.

"Yep, one hundred percent."

They exited the car and walked across the gravel to the main entrance.

"Keep your head down," he said, "but don't make it obvious, pretend you've spotted something on the ground or something." They weren't going to bother with gloves as neither of their prints were in the system.

She pointed at the ground, and they both looked down at the same time they entered the front door. Three customers glanced their way. There was no one behind the bar. They approached it, sat on a couple of stools and waited for the barman to appear.

It was a couple of minutes before Peter arrived and apologised for the delay. "Sorry, I was making a start in the cellar, we've got a delivery coming in the morning. I'll finish it off later. I wasn't expecting any latecomers. What can I get you, folks?"

"Two brandies, one with ice, thanks," Tim said, adding a deep timbre to his voice.

The barman served the drinks and began tidying the bar, collecting the dirty glasses. Over the next ten minutes, the other three customers drifted off, bidding Peter a merry farewell as they left.

"This is it." Tim said out of the corner of his mouth.

"Yep, bring it on."

"All right, folks. There's no need to rush. I can trust you by yourselves for a few minutes, can't I? While I finish off getting the cellar ready."

"Of course you can, mate. Want to lock the door in case anyone else comes in?"

"Yep, if that's okay with you." Peter bolted the door at the top. "Give me a shout when you leave."

Tim patted his stomach. "Eh, I could give you a hand down there if you want. I'm an ex-landlord myself, hence the rotund figure."

"Would you mind? I'm up against it, we've been really busy the last couple of days, and the staff have been dropping like flies. I haven't had the time to get things shipshape down there, you know what the draymen are like, impatient buggers at the best of times."

"You'll be all right here, chick, won't you?" Tim asked.

"Of course. I could clean up the bar a little for you, if you wanted me to. Anything to lend a hand." She made a point of using a high-pitched voice.

"No, you're all right, love. I've got a cleaner coming early in the morning. I'll get you another drink, though, if your fella is going to help me."

"You're too kind. Thank you."

Peter swept behind the bar, poured Miranda a larger measure than he'd served the first time, and then he motioned for Tim to join him.

"Be back soon." Tim pecked Miranda on the cheek.

"Good luck," she whispered.

DOWN IN THE CELLAR, Peter issued Tim with instructions on which barrels to shift into position first. Tim huffed and puffed, wasn't used to heavy manual work like this. "Right, that's done, what else?"

Peter turned his back to study the area. Tim took his opportunity, picked up an empty bottle lying at his feet and smacked it over Peter's head. The heavy-set man staggered forward, clutching a hand to his head.

He spun around and shouted, "What the fuck is your game?"

Tim picked up another bottle by its neck and tapped the bottom on the rim of one of the barrels he'd just shifted.

"Oh, that's the way you want to play it, is it? Well, bring it on, punk." Peter raised his arms to the side, and his chest expanded.

Tim gulped at the sheer size of the man. He reached down again and grabbed another bottle, but Peter cottoned on to what his intentions were. He let out a huge roar and flew at Tim. Tim took a step back to give himself more room and time to prepare his weapons for the attack. He hit the second bottle on a nearby shelf that gave it a pronounced jagged edge. Peter roared and bowed his head to ram Tim in the stomach. Tim swung the bottles back and forth, slicing into Peter's arms, head and shoulders. His attacker screamed out and backed up a few paces to confront him.

"Why, you fucking no-mark. You're going to pay for that."

"Yeah, come on then, big boy. I've got plenty more moves where they came from. Just because you're built like a Sherman tank, don't think you can frigging outsmart me."

"If this is about money, we can figure something out. The takings haven't recovered since the pandemic, but they're getting there. I've got money in the safe. Walk away now and that'll be the end of it."

"It's not! This is about so much more than money. This is about respect, or lack of it in your case."

Peter's brow furrowed. "Eh? You're not making any sense."

"The way you treat women is abysmal."

The man mountain shook his head. "Nope, I've got no idea what you're talking about."

"Denying it isn't going to get you out of this hole either."

"Read my lips, cocksucker. I'm not denying anything because I haven't got a scooby doo what you're going on about."

"The women in your life, you make them suffer."

Peter shook his head and growled. "My mother and sister? This is about them?"

"No, arsehole. Don't try to be clever with me. Your lovers, girlfriends and those you've had long-term commitments with."

"Bollocks. I've only had one in the last five years or so. She drove me frigging nuts. When I dumped her, I swore to myself I'd never get involved with another woman. I'm ten times happier alone."

"What was her name?"

Peter shrugged. "It's insignificant. I can't remember her sodding name. Why?"

"Because that woman was my sister."

The man mountain wiped away the blood that had dripped down his forehead and into his eyes. "So? What's this got to do with me? The last time I saw her was over five years ago, and here you are now, attacking me for going out with her. Why?"

"Because you and the other men she has been involved with since need to be taught a lesson in manners. You've all treated her appallingly."

"What about it? If, like you say, there have been others since she went out with me and we've all treated her the same, maybe, just maybe, you should take something from that."

"Meaning what?"

"Maybe it's that bitch of a sister of yours with the problem, not us men. Have you considered that, mate?"

The rage rose from within, and Tim glared at the bastard. "She's a beautiful woman, maybe a little misunderstood at times, but that's down to the way you and the other waste-of-space fuckers have treated her."

"Oh right, you keep telling yourself that, buddy. Maybe if you say it often enough you'll start to believe it." He pointed at his temple. "From what I can remember of her, she had a screw loose." Peter said what he had to say and then grunted after he took a whack across the head from behind. He toppled to the floor.

"I told you to stay upstairs and leave this to me," Tim shouted at Miranda. He noticed her eyes were glazed over with hatred and determination.

"No, you're taking too long down here. I've come to lend a hand. I want this bastard finished off for good. He ruined my life."

Peter groaned and held a hand to the back of his head. "What the...?"

Miranda held up one end of a rope and shook it out. She unravelled the knot near the end. "Let's tie him up. Quickly now, before he recovers," she ordered.

Her brother jumped into action and bound Peter's hands behind him. "Help me move him to an upright position."

Between them, they pulled and heaved their prisoner and propped him up against the shelves. The bottles jiggled above his head.

Tim looked down at the man and let out a satisfied laugh. "You won't be getting out of that one in a hurry, mate."

Peter, still a bit dazed from the whack Miranda had dished out, glared at each of them. "Still as ugly as ever, Miranda. I can see it's you now, even with that shitty disguise."

She kicked him hard in the calf. He cried out. She did it again for good measure.

"What now?" Miranda asked.

"Now, we have some fun," Tim replied.

They both laughed wildly, much to Peter's obvious disgust. He struggled to try to free himself, and one of the bottles above landed on his head. "Fuck. Do what you have to do and let this nightmare end," he pleaded, his head sinking onto his chest.

Tim smiled at his sister. "Nice of him to give us his permission." He jabbed one of the bottles into Peter's left bicep.

Miranda smiled, took the other bottle Tim was holding out to her and jabbed it into Peter's right arm.

He cried out and rolled his head from side to side through the pain.

Tim and Miranda paused and took in the man's agony for a second or two, then Tim aimed the bottle at the fleshy part of Peter's thigh, the glass piercing the material easily. The landlord yelled out, and the blood spurted, covering everything in its path for around three feet, including Tim's hand which he wiped down his trousers.

"Ooo… I liked that, let me have a go." Miranda stuck the bottle into the man's other thigh and quickly jumped back, aware of what would happen.

Tim watched his sister. She seemed fascinated by the way the blood arced out of their prisoner's leg and through the wound peeking out from the torn fabric.

"What great fun this is. Who knew torture could be beneficial to one's health?" Tim quipped.

"Not to his, that's for sure." Miranda chortled. "Where shall we aim for next?"

Tim took a step forward and thrust the bottle into Peter's neck. A weakened cry escaped Peter's lips.

Miranda quickly followed suit, and Peter cried out again. His head lolled to one side, blood escaping his lips. By now, his clothes were completely covered in the red fluid, too.

"Looks like he's on his way out. I want to finish him off. Please can I finish him off, bro?"

Tim nodded. "Be my guest. A stab to the chest should do it."

Miranda smiled and blew a kiss at him. She stepped forward again and thrust the bottle into Peter's chest, not once, twice, or three times, but dozens of times until Tim placed his arms around her and pulled her away.

"Hey, sis, he's gone now, and you seem to be enjoying that too much. Come on, let's get out of here."

They dropped the bottles and ran up the stairs hand in hand, giggling like naughty teenagers on their first date.

"Don't forget to dip your head as we leave the pub," he said.

"Will do."

Tim unlocked the door and opened it, allowing his sister to leave before him. He then slammed the door shut behind him, and they walked casually to the car, arm in arm.

Inside the vehicle, they high-fived each other. Tim wiped a smear of the man's blood from his sister's face and then kissed the spot. "I hope this aids your recovery, Miranda, it should also prove how much I love you. Not all men are the same, you know."

Miranda smiled and touched a hand to his face. "You've gone above and beyond to show how much you care about me. I will be eternally grateful for you giving me this opportunity to punish these men."

"It's not over yet. We still have more work to do."

"We're on the right track, though, and I feel a hundred times better than I did a few weeks ago."

He started the engine and noticed out of the corner of his eye his sister running a finger over the scars on her wrists. It choked him up to think how he would have felt if she'd succeeded in her mission to end her life.

CHAPTER 8

When the phone rang, Sam was having a lazy day—it was Saturday after all, and supposedly her weekend off. She was out with Sonny at the park which was full to bursting with like-minded people treating their dogs to a run around.

"Hello, DI Sam Cobbs."

"Forgive me for calling you on your weekend off, ma'am, but the pathologist has requested you to attend a crime scene with him."

"He has? Isn't anyone else available?" Sam kept a close eye on Sonny who was approaching a Yorkshire terrier on a lead. "Sonny, here boy. Sorry about that, I'm at the park with my overenthusiastic pooch."

"That's okay, ma'am, I have one of those myself, so I completely understand. As to your question, to be honest with you, I haven't tried anyone else as per the pathologist's instructions. Would you rather I see if anyone else can attend the scene?"

"No, I'll go. What's the location?"

"It's at The Flying Horse at Barepot."

"Okay. You're going to have to give me a little while to sort out dog-sitting for my pup. Sorry, you don't need to know that."

"I'll tell the pathologist to expect you within the hour, would that be okay?"

"Perfect." Sam ended the call and, in a panic, not wanting to put an extra burden on her neighbour's shoulders, looking after Sonny for yet another day, she rang her sister, Crystal. "Hi, it's me. Are you busy?"

"I will be in five minutes, I have someone browsing the window display. I have a feeling she's going to enter the shop soon. What's up?"

"No, you're too busy. I'll cope."

"For what? Don't go. What's wrong, Sam?"

"I've been called into work and I'm worried about leaving Sonny alone at the house. I have no idea how long I'm going to be."

"Shit! I'd have him here, but dogs and bridal gowns aren't a good match. If he cocked his leg up one of these beauties, that could wipe out my profit for the month."

"No, I wouldn't dream of expecting you to have him there. I'll give Mum a shout. Sorry to bother you. Good luck."

"No, wait. Ring Vernon instead. He loves spending time with Sonny and he's off injured today, so no match to attend."

"Would he? That'll be cool. I'll ring him now. Thanks, love."

Sam dialled her brother-in-law's number. He was a foot-baller for Carlisle United. The phone rang four times; patience wasn't a strong point of hers. Sam was about to hang up when a breathless Vernon answered. "Hi, Vernon, it's Sam."

"Hey, you. Long time no speak. How are you?"

115

"I'm fine. I hear you're not faring too well, though, what's wrong?"

"Pulled a ligament in my right ankle. Physio reckons I'll be up and about in a month or so. Pain in the arse, it is, I'm trying to keep fit and failing massively. Enough about me, how are you, sweetheart, you know, after that tosser walking out on you?"

Sam sniggered. "I'm doing surprisingly well, actually. I'm after a favour, Vernon."

"Go on. Hit me with it. If I can help, you know I will. You're my favourite sister-in-law after all."

Sam tutted. "I'm your *only* sister-in-law. I've just received a call to attend a crime scene. I was wondering if you wouldn't mind looking after Sonny for me."

"Bloody hell, I'd love it. The boredom is doing my head in. Can you drop him off? I can't drive, otherwise I'd come and get him."

"Not a problem. I'll shoot home, grab his food, bed and a few toys and be with you in about twenty to thirty minutes, how's that?"

"Whenever. Can you bring that tugging toy with you?"

"I'll do that. Do you need me to stop off for anything else en route?"

"Nope, we're all pretty well stocked up around here. Crystal went shopping at Asda last night on the way home."

"She's amazing, you both are. You make a great team."

"That we do. I'll see you soon."

Sam prodded the End Call button and trotted over to where Sonny was trying to make friends with the Yorkie. "I'm so sorry. He's far too friendly sometimes."

"That's all right, dear, no harm done. If Teddy didn't like him, he would have snapped his nose off by now. Fierce little one at the best of times, that's why I keep him on the lead."

Sam attached the leash to Sonny's collar. "Come on, you

tyke. We're off to Uncle Vernon's now." Sonny's head flicked from side to side; he adored Vernon. "Thanks for understanding, enjoy the rest of your walk," she said to the old lady.

"You, too, dear. It was nice to meet you."

"You, too," she called over her shoulder.

Sam scanned the park again but left disappointed. She had been hoping to see Rhys at the park, but it wasn't to be. It had been a while since they had laid eyes on each other, she had missed him, however, not enough to give him a call. Something was preventing her from taking the plunge, she couldn't put her finger on what. She trotted home and gathered Sonny's possessions together then put everything in the boot of her car and went back inside to collect Sonny. He sat alert in the back seat, eyeing the direction she was going in and whimpered as they pulled into Vernon's road.

"All right, settle down, munchkin. I'm sorry for deserting you like this, I was hoping to spend some quality time with you to make up for leaving you with Doreen all week, but you know what they say about best laid plans. Still, I think you're going to have the best day ever being with Uncle Vernon, you know how much he loves you."

Sonny sat up and watched the road ahead. He spun around in circles once Sam had applied the handbrake.

"Come on, Sonny. Let's go see your pal."

Vernon was leaning against the doorframe at the front door of his semi-detached home. Any money he made from football he'd been wise enough to not only invest in the house but also to back Crystal in her bridal business, which they presumed would keep them going long after his football career was over. "I'd lend you a hand but I'm incapacitated at the mo, love."

"Don't worry. Go back inside, I'm fine."

She left Sonny in the back seat while she unloaded everything else she'd brought to keep him occupied during the day. Task completed, she collected her furry companion—his whining had increased since he'd spotted Vernon at the door. She placed a hand on either side of his face. "Now listen to me, mister, you calm down or Vernon will reconsider having you here today." Kissing him on the nose, she unhooked his harness and led him out of the car and into the house.

"I'm in the lounge. Let him off the lead, Sam."

"Okay, if you insist."

Sonny tore through the house.

She removed her shoes and followed him into the lounge to find him planted firmly on Vernon's lap, licking his face all over. "Stop that, Sonny."

"He's fine. I could do with another wash. Do you have time for a coffee?"

"I'm sorry, no. I've got to dump Sonny and run. Maybe later?"

"Count on it. How long are you going to be?"

Sam shrugged. "Your guess is as good as mine. I haven't got a clue what type of crime I'm attending, all I know is that the pathologist requested me personally."

"Oh, what it is to be popular. That's because he wants the best in the business."

Sam smiled. "If you say so. Now, don't let him run rings around you, you hear me? If he gets too much, send him to his bed to give you both a break."

"He'll be fine. You worry too much. Go, let us get reacquainted, it's been a while since we've spent any time together. I've missed him."

She raised an eyebrow. "I suspect the feeling is mutual. Thanks for this, Vernon, I owe you one."

"Nah, it's always a pleasure to have this one's company. Don't worry about us. You know he's safe with me."

"I do. I'll give you a ring when I can, let you know how long I'm likely to be."

"Whatever. Don't fret, it's not like I'm going anywhere. I'm grateful for the company."

Sam leaned over and gave Vernon a peck on the cheek then kissed Sonny on the nose.

"I'm glad you did it that way round." Vernon chuckled.

"Be good, Sonny."

Her dog settled into Vernon's lap and continued to lick his face.

"Eww... he can be so disgusting at times. I'll leave you to it. Have fun."

"We will. He'll probably watch you go from the window the minute he realises you're leaving him with me."

"Probably. Bye, and thanks again, Vernon." Sam shot out of the lounge and closed the door behind her. She stood by the car and peered over her shoulder to find Sonny up on his back legs, his front paws on the windowsill in the lounge, howling.

She blew him a kiss and slipped behind the steering wheel, determined not to look back again. *I hate leaving him another day, but what else can I do?*

MENTALLY EXHAUSTED AFTER A LONG, fraught week, Sam turned up at the crime scene and popped on a white protective suit and shoe covers before she showed her ID to the constable on guard at the door. He held out the Crime Scene Log for her to sign then she ventured inside the large pub. "Hello, anybody around?" she called out, after finding the pub empty.

"Ah, is that you, Sam? We're down in the cellar. The door is open, it's off to your right slightly."

Sam peered around the post in the centre of the room,

and there it was, the doorway leading to God knew what. She removed the shoe covers and left them in the evidence collection bag. Luckily, she'd had the foresight to bring a few pairs with her. At the bottom of the stairs, she covered her shoes and slipped on a pair of gloves to preserve any evidence in the cellar. Des and his team of technicians were in front of her. The camera clicked several times as she made her way towards the pathologist.

Standing alongside him, Sam gasped at the bloody mess confronting her. "Bloody hell."

"Indeed. A lot of anger fuelled this attack."

"And some." She surveyed the area and was shocked by the amount of blood covering every surface. "He wasn't just attacked, he was tortured. Any evidence anywhere?"

Des smiled and held up a couple of evidence bags, each containing a broken bottle. "Yes, with prints on. Whether those prints will match up to anyone on the database, that's a different story."

"Odds are they won't. Maybe that's why the killer left them behind, they're keen to mess with us."

"More than likely. Either way, the victim suffered an horrendous death, my guess would be a sustained attack."

"Who found him?" she asked.

"The drayman at around eight this morning. He thought it was odd that Peter, our victim, wasn't up and waiting for him. Finding the door open, he ventured into the pub and said the light was on in the cellar, acting like a beacon for him to follow. He came down here, saw the bloody mess and legged it back upstairs. That's when he rang the police. I'm surprised you weren't informed by the station."

"It's supposed to be my weekend off; maybe they contemplated ringing me but thought better of it."

"Hey, it's supposed to be my weekend off as well. The wife is livid, but what can we do? Work comes first, eh?"

"Sadly, I agree, for now. Whether I do something about that sad fact in the future… well, let's just say, I'm toying with changing that notion, let's leave it at that for now."

Des tilted his head. "Are you telling me you're getting pissed off with police work, Inspector?"

"I didn't say anything of the sort. Let me put it this way, I have a lot of aspects of my life that are crying out to be changed, and there could be a knock-on effect to other areas of my life." She let out a slight growl. "Did that even make sense?"

"It did. It sounds to me like you have a lot of soul-searching to do when you get some time off to do it." He cleared his throat. "If ever you need an outsider to talk to, don't hesitate to count on me, Sam."

Her eyes misted up. "Get away with you, I'm fine. Come on, let's get back to the matter in hand. What else can you tell me?"

"If you're sure?" Sam nodded. "Okay, because of the excessive amount of blood on the floor, upon our arrival we discovered two separate footprints. We've measured them, and neither of them matches the victim."

"You're telling me we're looking at two perps?" Sam searched the area to find the possible footprints. "Here and here?" She pointed at the markers on the floor, keeping her distance from the evidence.

"That's correct. We've taken photos and assessed them thoroughly. One of them has a distinctive tread, the other nothing, indicating they might be some type of trainers or deck shoes."

"Interesting. Anything else?"

"Over here." Des took a few paces to his right, expecting her to follow. He pointed at the floor. "More blood here, just a few drops."

"Could it be from the perps? If they were covered in the victim's blood, might it have dripped off them as they left?"

Des smiled. "Good to know you're thinking about this. Maybe that's the case. I'm inclined to believe the perps attacked the victim here first, possibly knocked him out with a blow and then dragged him to his resting place, shall we say?"

"You're telling me you think the victim was caught unaware by the perps?" She glanced around the area and noticed the hatch door where the barrels would be delivered, but as far as she could tell, there were no other access points apart from the cellar opening where they had entered.

"More than likely. Either someone was lying in wait down here for him or they followed him down the stairs."

Sam cradled her chin between her thumb and forefinger. "Hmm… maybe. Would he be likely to come down here while the pub was open?"

"Possibly. You're going to need to check with the staff, see if there was anyone else on duty last night. I'd be surprised if he was the only one working on a busy Friday night."

"You're presuming the pub was busy, not always the case these days," Sam retorted.

A female shouted from upstairs.

"I'll be back, we might get an answer to that question soon." She ran through the cellar and up the stairs. Again, pausing to change the covers on her shoes.

She found a female uniformed officer blocking a woman from entering the pub.

"Let me pass. I demand to know what the fuck is going on. Where's Peter? His car is outside, so where is he?"

Sam undid the zipper of her suit to search for her ID. "Hi, I'm Detective Inspector Sam Cobbs, and you are?"

"Katrina Moss. I work here."

"What's your role here, Katrina?"

"I'm the cleaner, plus I work a few shifts behind the bar at lunchtimes. You haven't answered my question, where's Pete?"

"Let's take a seat." Sam gestured to a picnic table just outside the front door.

"I don't have time to sit down, I need to get on with my work. What's going on? Please, you have to tell me. All this is sending me into a frenzy. My nerves are shot most days as it is, without all this shit to contend with."

"Please, listen to me and take a seat."

Katrina took one pace towards the seating area and stopped. "I've got a feeling I'm not going to like what you have to say."

"Please, sit down."

Reluctantly, the woman took a seat, and Sam slipped off her suit, deposited it in another evidence bag and sat opposite her.

Sam sucked in a breath and let it out slowly and then broke the unwanted news to Katrina. "It is with regret that I have to tell you we have found a body in the cellar."

Katrina gasped and cupped a hand over her mouth. Her eyes watered, and she shook her head vigorously. After a few moments, she dropped her hand and in a hushed voice asked, "Is it him? Pete?"

"As yet, we don't have an ID for the body. Could it be anyone else?"

"I don't know, do I? You're the one who has seen him, not me."

"I meant, does Pete run the pub alone or does he have a partner?"

"Alone. He was a one-man band. Committed to his work. Loved this place and dealing with the customers on a daily basis. I can't believe he's dead. Wait, the drayman is in his lorry over there, he's not usually here by the time I arrive.

Does he have something to do with Pete's death? Why haven't you arrested him? I'm sorry, I'm not trying to tell you how to do your job, it just seems a logical process to me."

"No need for you to apologise, it was the drayman who found him. The man is shaken up, I need to have a word with him in a moment. Are you all right? I know the news has probably come as a shock to you."

"Too right. It's bloody knocked me sideways, it has. Was it a burglary?" She pointed at the camera above the front door. "Have you viewed the cameras yet?"

It was the first time Sam had noticed the equipment, and knowing they were there lifted her spirits. "Not yet. I only arrived about five minutes ago. I've been down in the cellar with the pathologist, assessing the crime scene. Are there more cameras inside?"

"Yes, wait! Are you telling me it happened down there? No one is allowed in that area. It's Pete's domain. He takes, or should I say, took? He took pride in keeping that area in tiptop condition. Maybe he was down there preparing the cellar for the delivery today."

"Possibly. Would you know if he had any staff working alongside him last night?"

"Let me think." She paused and her brow furrowed. "Abby was supposed to be working. Do you want me to give her a call?"

"If you wouldn't mind."

Katrina dug into the bottom of her bag to retrieve her mobile. She scrolled through her screen and then tapped it. "Hey, Abby, yeah, it's me. Were you working last night...? Oh no, I'm so sorry to hear that, are you feeling better now, babe...? That's good... Yeah, I'm at work... Something is up, but I can't tell you what over the phone... Yeah, it's serious, the police are here. I'll give you a call when I can. Speak later." Katrina ended the call and placed her phone on the table. "She said she called in sick with a tummy bug. It's unusual for Abby, she never wags time off, so she must have been bad."

"I see. Would Pete likely try to replace her?"

"He doesn't have a lot of options, not these days. Since the pandemic and the government messing us about, he's had to lay off a lot of the staff. Therefore, he's had to up his game. Put in the extra hours to make up for the lost staff. He's been working flat-out for months now."

"That's very sad. Do you know anything about the cameras and working the equipment?"

"I can get by with it, at a push, I suppose. Do you want to have a look at it?"

"That would be fantastic. Let me grab a couple of suits, you can't go inside until we're properly dressed, we'll contaminate the crime scene. Where is the equipment?"

"In the storeroom behind the bar. Do you want me to show you the way?"

"Thanks."

After they donned a suit each, snapped on a pair of gloves and covered their shoes, Katrina led the way to a storeroom which was a lot tidier than Sam had been in at other pubs over the years.

"Nice and tidy, at least you can see where everything is," Sam noted.

"That's because Pete liked to know where everything was. If it was easily accessible then it saved time having to search for it. He organised the whole pub during the lockdown last year. Told me it was to save his sanity. He gave the inside of the pub a fresh lick of paint, too, like many other pubs in the area, I shouldn't wonder."

"I think you're right. Is this the equipment connected to the cameras?"

"Yes. You're going to have to be patient with me, I'm not

the best with technical stuff, my hubby will vouch for me there. I piss him off most days when I have trouble setting up the DVD recorder at home."

"I'm sure we'll be able to muddle through between us." Sam studied the machinery. "I see the disc is still running. It should be easy enough to stop and rewind it, at least I'm hoping that's the case." Sam stopped the disc and hit Rewind, then stopped it after a few seconds and pressed Play. The time in the corner of the screen said seven o'clock. She watched a man enter the pub and call out for Pete.

"That's the drayman," Katrina said.

"It is. Okay, let's go back." She pressed Rewind and stared at the same picture for what seemed like ages until a couple came into view. "The time is eleven thirty-three. It looks like the last members of the public leaving here."

"Hmm... can you go back a little? I don't see Pete anywhere."

Sam did as requested and rewound the disc, slowly this time.

"There, what the heck? Those two people have just come out of the cellar. Pete would never allow anyone to go down there, especially not strangers. What the heck went on down there?"

"Okay, try and remain calm, let's keep going backwards to see what happened. Maybe he invited them down there to have a look around."

Katrina turned to Sam and shook her head. "Never in a gazillion years. Even the staff are banned from that area. It's his pride and joy."

"Maybe they're other publicans and he was showing off?"

Katrina shook her head. "I don't know about that. You didn't know Pete like I did."

"All right, let's see what happens. Keep an eye open." Sam pressed Rewind again. "Is that Pete behind the bar?"

"Yes, that's him."

Now Sam had a positive ID for the victim, she let the disc play out. "He seems to be quite chatty with the couple."

"He's pouring the woman a brandy."

"Right, and now he's gone down to the cellar. The couple are chatting, they seem friendly enough. I can't see anyone else in the bar, is it usually quiet on a Friday night?"

"Hit and miss like any other night these days, hence Pete cutting down on the staff. I'm only still on the bar rota because I've worked for him for over five years as a cleaner. He took pity on me. I need the cash, since I lost my husband to that effing virus."

"Oh my, I'm so sorry to hear that." Sam's heart lurched for the woman; at least Chris was still alive. Or was he? The truth was, she didn't know one way or the other. Turning her attention back to the screen, she pointed out the male's movements towards the cellar. "He's following Pete down there." She jotted down the time in her notebook and watched on.

"Bloody hell, now that woman is going down there."

"Why would she go down there?"

"Your guess is as good as mine," Katrina replied. "Dodgy comes to mind."

Which was the assumption I already came to knowing what state Pete's body is in down in the cellar.

She fast forwarded the disc a little until the couple emerged from the cellar.

Katrina gasped. "Oh no, look at all that blood. Shit! What did they do to Pete?"

"I'm sorry you had to see that. It's obvious we're watching Pete's killers. Do you recognise them? I'll stop the disc now. Any idea how to make a copy?"

"No, I've never seen them before. Take it with you, I don't care about you having a copy. All I want is for you to find

127

these bastards and punish them for taking Pete's life. Jesus, that image is going to live with me for the rest of my days."

"I'm sorry. Okay, if you're sure, we'll return it to you as soon as we can. Are you going to be all right?"

"No, never again, not after this. My whole world has collapsed now Pete is gone. Bang goes my job, my income. I'm barely making ends meet at the moment as it is, and now this. Sorry, that makes me sound so selfish when Pete has lost his life." Katrina broke down and cried.

Sam resisted the urge to comfort her. "I'm so sorry. You're looking out for yourself, not being selfish at all. Can I call anyone? A friend or family member?"

"My brother, but he's at work. No, don't worry, I'll be fine. Would it be all right if I made myself a cup of coffee in the kitchen?"

"Yes, do that, I'm going to need you to take it outside, back to the table. Before you leave, I need you to take your suit off at the exit and place it in the same bag where I put mine. I know it's a rigmarole but it's procedure. I need to have a word with the pathologist."

"Thank you for your kindness. Do you want me to make anyone else a coffee while I'm at it?"

"I'd love one. Don't worry about the tech team, they'll have a break when it suits them."

They left the room together and went in different directions. Sam renewed her shoe covers, tucked the used pair in the evidence bag and descended. At the bottom, she called out, "Des, I have some information for you, all right if I come over?"

"Sure, just be careful where you're stepping."

Sam followed the trail of the evidence steps through all the markers on the floor and stood alongside Des who was standing back, observing the victim, while a member of his team took photos.

"What information?" Des asked.

"I've just viewed the CCTV footage. A couple, a man and a woman, were visible on the disc."

"That's excellent news. Can you see their faces?"

"Yes. I'm going to take the disc back to the station, see if I can get some clear shots of the suspects. If that's possible, I'll run them through the system. I have a good feeling about this one."

"You seem pretty buoyant about it. We're just doing the necessary and then we'll make a move. Was the woman all right? Who was she?"

"The cleaner-cum-barmaid, she's pretty shaken up. She's given me the victim's name as Peter. I'll find out his surname before I let her go home."

"Poor woman, at least she didn't witness what we've seen down here. She'd be a darn sight worse if she had."

"You're not kidding. The suspects were covered in the vic's blood, that's what set her off, seeing that on the footage."

"Shit! I'm not surprised they were covered. They hit some of the major arteries, hence the amount of arterial bleeding everywhere. Was that intentional? At this stage, I'm not sure."

"It doesn't have the feel of a professional kill. I saw the interaction between Pete and the suspects, he seemed very friendly towards them."

"It's not uncommon for suspects to try and get on a victim's good side and then kill them, we all know that's a possibility in this game."

"So true. The thought of that man being confronted by two psychopaths and not being able to escape their clutches sends a bloody shiver up my spine."

Des squeezed her shoulder. "Don't think too long or too hard about it."

"I'd better get back upstairs before I have a meltdown. Not sure why I'm feeling so damned emotional these days."

"I know why, you would too, if you took a step back and truly thought about it, Sam. I was wrong to call you. Why don't you ring your partner, tell him to take over from you and go home? You have a lot on your plate at the moment."

She waved the idea away with a limp hand. "I'm fine, don't worry about me. I'd rather be at work, keeping myself occupied. I'll let you know when I plan to leave."

"You do that. My advice would be not to push yourself too hard, Sam Cobbs. Listen to me, I'm a doctor."

Gulping loudly, she said, "Do I have to remind you what type of doctor you are?"

"Nope, I'm glad you picked up on my implication. Think on, Sam, be kind to yourself, I would truly hate for you to end up on the slab before me."

Her eyes widened. "Blimey, you can be such a charmer at times. I'm out of here, while I still have a pulse." She smiled, and Des returned her smile before turning his attention to a member of his team who had appeared beside him to ask a question.

Upstairs, she replaced the shoe covers once more and went outside to sit with Katrina who had her head bowed as she stared at the mug nestled between her fingers. "How are you?"

A hand left her mug and covered her chest. "Bugger, you scared the shi... sorry, the life out of me. I made you a cup."

"Oops, I apologise. I should have considered you were lost in thought. Thanks for the drink. Are you all right?"

"I think so. My mind is reeling, seeing all the blood over those... people. I know I haven't seen the state Peter's in, and I wouldn't want to, but that doesn't stop my mind working overtime. That poor man, he didn't deserve to die, no one does. Why do people have to take someone else's life anyway? If they don't like what's going on about them, bugger off to a different part of the country or something. Why kill someone?"

"It's always a hard question to answer. There are so many different motives and reasons behind someone robbing another person of their last breath, it beggars belief sometimes. It's better not to dwell on it for too long, otherwise it can make you as bitter and twisted as the killers in the long run."

"Twisted, yes, that seems a fitting and accurate appraisal of the bastards. May they rot in Hell for killing Peter when he's done nothing wrong."

"Ah, but do we know he's done nothing wrong? How well did you *really* know him?"

Katrina's eyebrows rose. "I suppose you have a point."

Sam took a sip from her mug. "Did he have any relatives in the area? Was he in a relationship perhaps?"

"No, he was what I call a loner. Never spoke about his family much. He moved up here around ten years ago from the Midlands somewhere, I think. Don't quote me on that, though. He has had a few girlfriends since I've known him, nothing that major, not really."

"Thanks, I'll do some digging when I get back to the station. Finish your drink and get yourself off. Sorry, what was Pete's surname? And do you have a key to the pub?"

"Richmond was his surname. And yes, only Pete and I had a key."

"Sounds like he put a lot of trust in you."

Katrina sniffled. "I like to think he did."

Suddenly, Sam remembered the drayman, sitting in his lorry outside. "Excuse me a moment." She sprinted across the car park and smiled at the driver who was glaring down at her. "Hello, I'm sorry to keep you waiting so long. As you can imagine, there was a lot of information relating to the crime to sift through with the pathologist."

He opened his door and climbed down, then rubbed his hand across his neck. "Don't worry, I had a feeling you'd be tied up in there for a while. Poor bloke, I've never witnessed anything so gruesome in all my fifty-odd years on this earth. I'm Ted by the way. Ted Wilson."

"Hi Ted, I'm DI Sam Cobbs. You're right, not pleasant at all. Did you see anyone else hanging around when you arrived?"

He shook his head. "No one. You didn't think the killer would still hang around, did you?"

"It has been known. Some psychos get off from watching the activity surrounding a crime scene they've created."

"Wow, is that even a thing? Bloody wackos. Anyway, no, the car park was empty, apart from Pete's car over there. I know it's his because it broke down once when I was delivering and I helped him get it on the road again."

"That was nice of you. You got on with him then?"

"Yeah, he was a likeable chap. Expert beer handler, liked his cellar to be in perfect condition every day. He would have been freaking out about the mess down there... Jesus, I can't believe I said that, dumb bloody statement at the best of times, let alone when the landlord has just lost his life."

"Don't worry. It's not uncommon for folks' tongues to run away from them when something of this nature occurs."

"I suppose it's the shock."

"Probably. Just to get things straight in my head, you arrived at seven, was it?"

"Yes, my usual time or thereabouts. It was unusual for Pete not to have the hatch open for me, so I went inside looking for him and that's when I found him, covered in blood. Dead."

"It must have been awful for you to find him like that."

"It was. I'm not one for running usually, but I can tell you,

I could have beaten Usain Bolt out of that cellar if he'd been down there."

Sam smiled in spite of the gravity of the situation. "And you got back in your lorry and called the police from there?"

"That's right. Jumped in and ensured all the doors were locked before I did anything else. The person had to be a bloody nutter. Do you reckon the poor bloke was tortured for hours down there? Seems that way to me."

"I won't know the details of the attack until the pathologist has conducted his post-mortem, but I'm inclined to believe it was definitely a sustained attack."

Ted shook his head. "It's mind-numbing to think someone can do that much harm to another human being. I know you hear all sorts on the TV, and we're desensitised to it somehow, but seeing something like this in the flesh, it makes you wonder what type of world we're living in these days." He glanced over his shoulder and leaned in. "I have a theory if you want to hear it."

Sam leaned in, too, mimicking him, and said, "What's that?"

"It's controversial."

"Go on."

"I blame the foreigners they're letting into the country. You want to hear some of the stories I've heard over the years from other drivers, especially the ones who have to cross the Channel. I tell you, those guys risk their own lives on a daily basis. Most of them have been beaten up by immigrants desperate to get to our shores. That's all they know, some of them. Let's face it, most of them are from war-torn places, they no longer know how to live a peaceful life, and here we are, letting the buggers into the country and giving them houses that our own people are crying out for. Where's the sense in that? I was always told to take care of your own before looking after outsiders. Have you any idea how many homeless ex-soldiers are living on our streets?"

"In my opinion, you shouldn't really be saying things like this publicly. We have a duty of care to consider."

"Duty of care? At what cost? You think old Pete in there was bothered about duty of care, while someone was slicing him up? I know I go over the top with my views at times, I'm just saying, the violence is escalating yearly in this country, it's about time the government stepped back and took a good look at itself for allowing unknowns to live amongst us. Where are the visas? Who knows the background of these people? Do we know their police records? Have they been in prison? If so, for what?"

Sam raised her hand. "That debate is for another day, Ted. For now, I need to prioritise this case."

"Sorry, you're right. Me spouting my mouth off about things we're not able to change isn't helping much. What do you need from me?"

"I'm going to need to take a statement. Not now, within the next few days, if that's okay?"

"Sure. I'm always willing to help the boys and girls in blue. You'll be wanting my address."

Sam poised her pen and notebook and jotted down the address he gave her.

"I'm local, as in Whitehaven."

"And your phone number?"

He supplied that, and she flipped her notebook shut. "That concludes our interview. Thanks so much for hanging around to speak with me. The station will be in touch to make the arrangements about the statement."

"Thanks. Good luck, I hope you find the little shit who killed Pete, soon."

Sam held up her crossed fingers and headed back to where she found Katrina downing the remains of her drink.

"Are you off now?" Sam asked.

The woman glanced up, a glimmer of a smile pulling at her dry, pale lips. "Yes, there's nothing I can do around here, is there?"

"Can you give us your key? I'll get forensics to drop it off at the station and ask one of the uniformed officers to get it back to you by the end of the day. I'll need your address."

Katrina gave her details and the key and walked away with her head bowed.

I feel for her. I hope she's going to be okay. Maybe I'll give her a call later to make sure.

Sam donned yet another suit and set of covers, cursing the number that had been used already, and entered the pub again. She stood at the top of the stairs and called, "Des, can you hear me?"

He came to the bottom. "What's up?"

"I'm going to the station now, to get things started. Do you need me for anything else?"

"Not as far as I know. Take care. I'll be in touch. Needless to say, the PM reports on the other two cases might be somewhat delayed."

"Don't worry about it. I'll be in touch soon."

BACK AT THE STATION, Sam had just collected a coffee and was adding the new victim's name to the whiteboard when her mobile rang. She removed it from her pocket and glanced at the name on the screen. "Hello, you. What are you up to, partner?"

"I was in your neck of the woods and thought I'd pop in for a coffee."

"Hmm... in other words, you're checking up on me."

"I'm mortally offended by that remark."

"Which happens to be the truth. Anyway, it doesn't matter, I'm not at home."

"Oh? In that case, I'm sorry to disturb you if you're out visiting someone."

"I have been, the last few hours, visiting a dead body."

"What are you talking about?"

"I'm at work. Des requested I join him at a crime scene, a gruesome one at that."

"Why didn't you call me? I would have come in to be with you. It's not too late."

"No, there's no point in both of us giving up our day off."

"Are you going to tell me about it?"

"A landlord was murdered in his cellar. There was blood everywhere."

Bob sighed. "Any witnesses as to who committed the crime? Could the pubs be the connection?"

"No witnesses, not as such. What I do have is CCTV footage of the perps. One male, one female. The pub angle might be something we need to check into later."

"Okay, that's it, I'm coming in. Whether you agree or not. Two heads are better than one, and I'm only around the corner, so no great hardship."

"No, wait. What about Abigail?"

"She's shopping with Milly. It was her suggestion that I should pop in and see you. They'll be hours, so I won't be missed."

"Okay, if you insist."

"Put the kettle on... umm... you know what I mean."

She laughed. "I'll get you a drink lined up. Wait, will you be passing a baker's on the way in?"

"You know damn well I will be. What do you want?"

"A sandwich of sorts and maybe an iced bun for afters. I'll settle up with you when you get here."

"Your wish is my command. Give me ten minutes."

Sam ended the call, a warm fuzzy glow filling her insides at the prospect of Bob joining her for a few hours.

Fifteen minutes later, she was on her way back with two drinks in her hand when Bob breezed into the room. He popped the brown paper bag containing her lunch on the desk closest to the whiteboard.

"You're fantastic. I don't tell you that nearly enough."

He frowned. "Umm… correction, you never tell me. I got you a tuna and mayo on brown and I went the whole hog and bought you a cream slice; they were too tempting sitting in the cabinet by the till, I struggled to resist."

"A man after my own heart. Let's eat this before we start discussing the case."

"You know me, I don't need telling twice where food is concerned."

Sam dived into the bag and removed its contents. "I take it this large baguette has your name on it?"

"Correct, plus a cream slice. Should fill a hole."

"Blimey, I wouldn't need to eat the rest of the weekend if I ate all that."

They chatted while they chomped their way through the lunch. Sam surprised herself by eating every last morsel, and then she realised it was the first she'd eaten since fixing herself an omelette for the previous night's dinner.

"Yummy. Thanks, Bob, that all went down a treat."

"Let's hope it stays down." He screwed up the paper bag and aimed it at his bin. "Bullseye. Okay, hit me with it." He raised a hand. "No, wait."

Sam had opened her mouth and slammed it shut again. "Why? What's going on?"

Bob sat upright, placed a hand to his chest and let out the largest belch she'd ever heard. "That's better."

She placed her hands over her face and shuddered. "How

the hell does that beautiful wife of yours put up with you? A pig has more manners than you do."

"Steady on there. As my old nan used to say, it's better out than in. Can you imagine the damage that could have caused to my insides if I hadn't let it out?"

"Enough of your disgusting habits. I'm already regretting you being here."

"What? After I've just supplied you with lunch? There's gratitude for you."

"Getting back to business before I lose my sanity altogether..." She then spent the next five minutes running through what she'd been confronted with once she'd arrived at the crime scene. Then she dug into her handbag and removed the disc. "I'll leave you to fire up the machine."

"I wouldn't mind another coffee," he called over his shoulder.

Sam bought the coffees, and Bob had the equipment set up by the time she had returned. She got out her notebook and flicked back to the times she had noted down, and Bob searched through the disc.

"What the? They're there, as plain as day. Do you think he knew them? What did the cleaner say?"

"She didn't recognise them. They seemed friendly enough with Pete. You wait until you see the state of their clothes. Fast forward a little. Wait, that's it."

They sat in silence to view the disc.

Eventually, Bob whistled. "The brass neck of the fuckers. They walked out of the pub covered in his frigging blood. They've got to be psychos to do that, haven't they?"

"Yep, I agree. Granted, it would have been pitch-black outside, therefore no one would have seen the blood on their clothes. What we need to do is try and print off an image of the fuckers, one that's good enough to put through the system."

"You think they're going to be on it? Didn't you say Des had discovered fingerprints and footprints in the cellar?"

"That's right. We've got to be hopeful that something will show up."

Bob shook his head. "I get the impression that these guys are toying with us. All this is intentional."

Sam frowned and stared at the screen. "Are you saying what I think you're saying? That you think these are disguises?"

Bob shrugged. "Unless you've got a better idea? All right, here, they're doing their very best to hide their faces from the cameras, but maybe they didn't notice the camera filming them from behind the bar. In my opinion, they're amateurs with one main ambition."

"To mess with our heads?"

"You've got it."

Bob pressed a few buttons. The image of the man on the screen improved well enough to get a viable printout. Bob handed her the image. Something sparked in her mind and made her tear across the room to the whiteboard.

"What are you thinking?" Bob asked.

"It might be a long shot, but take a look at this."

Bob stood beside her. She held up the photo that Bob has just sourced and placed it on the whiteboard next to the CCTV image of the man they knew as Ian from the first crime.

"Whoa! That's some resemblance. If it's him, he's definitely wearing a disguise in one of the photos, maybe in both of them," Bob said.

Sam sank onto the desk behind her. "What if the two crimes are connected?"

Bob stared at the whiteboard and folded his arms. "What if all three cases are connected and we've got a couple of psycho serial killers on our hands?"

"Wait, we can't say that. We have no proof along those lines."

"That's where forensics come in. If the bastards have left fingerprints and shoe prints all over the crime scene from this morning, and forensics find any trace evidence at the other crime scenes, then surely that's going to give us the answer."

"I'll get on to Des, see what he thinks." Sam ran a hand over her face.

"Don't let him try and talk you out of it. Trust me on this one, I think I'm right. While you make the call, I'm going to go over what evidence has been located at the other crime scenes."

"Wait, there was a tyre print at the second scene. We could view any cameras in the area of the pub, ANPRs and CCTV, see if we can spot the car and match it to the tyre."

"Now we're cooking on gas. Let's see what we can dig up."

"I'll call Des first." Sam dipped into her office, where she felt more comfortable making calls, and rang Des's mobile. "Sorry to disturb you, Des, it's Sam, can you talk?"

"I can make an exception for you, what's up?"

"I'm going through the video footage with Bob back at the station, and we believe we've sussed something out."

"You have piqued my interest with that notion. How can I help?"

"We're wondering if all three crimes could be linked. We have a possible suspect/person of interest we're keen to speak to from the first crime scene, the man who was out drinking with Brian Coltman, who accompanied him back to the boat."

"A link?"

"Sorry, yes, after viewing the footage of the two perps from the pub, there's a definite resemblance in the male, to this Ian we're trying to locate. And you have fingerprints and footprints belonging to the perps at the pub today."

"Ah, I see what you're getting at. You want me to double-check and triple-check with forensics to see if there were any possible foot or fingerprints found on the boat which might be of use in making the link."

"Yes, that's it. Hang on, plus you mentioned a tyre tread print from the second scene."

"That's correct. Have you got anything to match it to?"

"Not yet. We're in the process of searching the cameras around the area of the pub to see if we can locate the suspects and identify what vehicle they're driving."

"Excellent. One question."

"Go on."

Des paused and then asked, "Would the killers be so sloppy as to leave such an obvious trail?"

"Another assumption we've come to is that maybe the perps are toying with us."

"It's not beyond the realms of possibility, I suppose. Okay, leave all this with me. I'll get back to you as soon as I have anything of use."

"Cheers, Des." Sam hung up, sat back in her chair and closed her eyes, reflecting on what would probably lay ahead of them.

"Everything all right?" Bob asked from the doorway.

"Just psyching myself up."

"I know what you mean, so many angles for us to check on, it's going to be nigh on impossible for the two of us to come up with the goods."

"What are you suggesting? That we spoil the team's R and R over the weekend?"

"It's something we should consider if we want to catch these fuckers."

"Let's take a rain check on that for now and muddle

through just the two of us for a couple of hours. If we find ourselves struggling then I promise I'll hit the phones and request their company. They've worked flat-out all week, they deserve their time off."

Bob raised an eyebrow and pointed at Sam and then himself. "And we don't? Anyway, we'd better crack on, I'm only here for a few hours, don't forget."

"I know." She sprang to her feet and followed him back into the incident room. "What about the footage, have you requested it?"

"Yep, they're short-staffed, or should I say they're running a skeleton staff at the weekend, but they've promised to get back to me by midday, at the latest on Monday."

"Not ideal, but I suppose it'll have to do. We could go back to The Flying Horse and have a hunt around ourselves. See if there are any cameras from which we could likely obtain any footage, what do you reckon?"

"I was thinking along the same lines... What? Don't give me that look as though you don't believe me."

UNDER FIFTEEN MINUTES LATER, Sam parked the car in a spot closest to the side of the pub. "There's only one way in and out."

Bob leaned forward to get a better view of the surrounding buildings and pointed at a shop opposite. "It's disguised, but I reckon that's a camera lurking just under the second-floor window. Can you see it?"

"Where? I can't see a damn thing. I need to get my eyes tested again, I'm sure they've got worse recently."

"Not helpful when we're on the lookout for suspects, or vital clues for that matter, boss."

"I apologise. If you think it's a camera then we should go and speak to the owner or manager of the shop."

They waited for several cars and a motorbike to pass and then crossed the road. The shop was a typical corner shop, selling mainly groceries. It also had a small post office at the rear.

Sam approached the man with receding hair and spectacles standing behind the till. "Hello, sir. I'm DI Cobbs, and this is my partner, DS Jones."

His smile dropped. "The police? Has someone reported me? I only had a go at those boys because I could sense they were up to no good."

Sam raised her hand to stop him. "No, it's nothing like that."

He peered over his shoulder at the pub. "Ah, I'm such an idiot. Is this to do with you lot being over at the pub? Katrina popped in on her way home, she told me the sad news about Pete."

"That's correct. We were wondering if you had a camera on the premises."

"Of course I do." He pointed at the sign in the window, something else Sam had neglected to see on her way in. "I find the sign is as much of a deterrent as the camera itself. It's probably me talking bullshit, though…" His voice tapered off at the end, and he strained his neck to see if there were any other customers in the shop who'd entered behind them.

"Good to see someone taking security seriously. Would it be all right if we view the disc from last night?"

His clenched fist bashed the side of his head. "Now why didn't I think about that? You'll be wanting to see what cars came and went during the evening, won't you?"

"Precisely."

"I can sort that out for you. I'll just close the shop for half an hour. Let me scribble down an apologetic note to keep the customers sweet." He searched for a scrap piece of paper under the till and wrote, *Back in thirty minutes. Sorry for the inconvenience.* "That should pacify them." He tore off a strip of Sellotape and attached it to the sheet of paper and then stuck it on the inside of the glass panel on the front door. After locking it, he rubbed his hands together and said, "Follow me. Let's see what we can find for you."

He led the way out through the back area to a stockroom filled with Zamba shelving. The room was fairly cool, and a fair amount of stock lined the shelves.

"Are you busy here?" Sam enquired.

"We have our moments. I try and see what special offers I can put on to entice the locals. It's mostly women who come through the doors, if I'm honest. Suits me, they're the ones who generally do the shopping anyway. And no, that's not a sexist comment, it's a fact."

Sam sniggered. "I bet. Even when men get around to doing the shopping, they tend to forget half of what they intend getting but always manage to remember a six-pack of beers."

"Never a truer word spoken. Right, let's sort this out for you. Is there a special time you want me to look for?"

Sam scratched her head and then flipped open her notebook. "Around eleven-thirty. If you aim for around eleven forty-five and we'll go from there."

"I'll do that."

He pressed the controls, and then images of the pub opposite filled the monitor. The picture was grainy in parts, but Sam thought they would be adequate judging by how well she could make out the Ford Ka that had just exited the car park. Bob nudged her and gave a thumbs-up.

She offered a weary smile. *Something has to come our way soon.* "Sorry, I didn't get your name."

"It's John Halls. You can call me Johnnie."

"We really appreciate you doing this for us, Johnnie."

144

"Nonsense. Anything to help old Pete out. He was a good guy once you got to know him. Not the type to take any shit from folks, though. I suppose he was a typical publican in that regard."

"But he was nice with it?" Sam clarified.

"Oh yeah, we all got on with him around here. I'll tell you one thing, he's going to be a massive loss to the community. The punters knew where they stood with him. He did a lot for charity, held a few quizzes where all the proceeds went to the local hospice. I don't know many publicans willing to do that sort of thing, not these days, after what the world has been through recently."

"Trying times, I agree. Good to hear he was the type to make a difference, sad to think someone dismissed that information and willingly ended his life."

"Are you saying whoever killed him was a local?" Johnnie asked.

Sam shrugged. "We're not sure. Hopefully, if we can identify the suspects' vehicle via your camera, we'll get a clearer picture."

He whizzed through the footage and stopped on a Vauxhall coming out of the car park. "That's old Ray, he lives up the road here but insists on driving everywhere, and yes, he's been known to drink and drive. We've all warned him about his careless attitude, but he's a stubborn old fool at the best of times."

Sam rolled her eyes. "What will it take for him to reconsider his dangerous actions, killing someone?"

"Well, he knocked down a dog last year and was presented with the vet's bill, which he duly paid. It hasn't stopped his careless behaviour one iota. The older he gets the more he seems to dig his heels in."

"That's terrible." Sam watched another vehicle leave the car park. "And this one?"

"That's Nick. He tends to sit at the bar all night with a half of mild for company."

Johnnie fast forwarded the disc and paused it when a light-coloured Peugeot came to a stop at the exit. Sam jotted down the number plate and raised her brow at Bob. "Seems too easy to me."

He nodded his agreement. "Far too easy. I bet we find it burnt out later."

"Do you think they're the ones guilty of killing Pete?" Johnnie asked, the colour draining from his previously flushed cheeks.

"Possibly. Do you recognise the car or the passengers?"

Johnnie zoomed in as much as possible on the passengers and shook his head. "I don't recognise them as locals at all. Can't say I've seen the car around here either. Sorry."

"It's fine. Would it be possible for you to give us a copy of the disc?"

"I'll get one for you now. Hard to imagine a woman being involved in such a monstrous crime."

Sam nodded and shuddered. "Yes, it is."

"Katrina said the couple were covered in Pete's blood. It must have been a vicious attack."

"It was. One of the worst I've seen. Hence the reason we're out here today, on our day off, gathering evidence."

"I take my hat off to you, not every copper would consider doing that."

"It's purely selfish reasons." Sam tucked her notebook in her jacket pocket. "The quicker we find the killers, the less work we'll be forced to do in the end."

"If your job is anything like mine regarding paperwork, I can totally understand where you're coming from. Sorry, I mean on the post office side of things."

"It is." Sam smiled.

Johnnie reached for a new disc and presented her with it

once he'd copied the contents over. "Here you go, I hope it helps."

"I'm sure it will. It's more than we had to go on five minutes ago, so it's got to count for something. We really appreciate your help."

"Always willing to help out when I can. I hope it proves worthwhile and you capture the guilty bastards soon."

Johnnie showed them back through to the shop where he unlocked the door to let them out.

"Thanks again, Johnnie."

"You're welcome."

Sam took a few steps and said to Bob, "Let's get back to the station and run the plate."

"What else? Are you going to call on the press and media for help in identifying them?"

Sam opened her car door and slipped inside. Bob got in beside her.

"It's a tough one," she said. "The last thing we want to do is scare them. I've had my share of chasing criminals all over these fells."

"I hear you on that one."

At around six, Sam called it a day and headed back to Vernon and Crystal's to pick up Sonny. Bob had left the station an hour earlier, once he'd received the call from Abigail to pick her and Milly up from their shopping expedition.

She had rung ahead, and Sonny was up at the window in the lounge, awaiting her arrival. Her heart skipped a beat when she saw his face light up.

Crystal opened the door and hugged her. "Hey, you look shattered. I've run it past Vernon; why don't you spend the night here with us? We could order in a Chinese. You're coming for lunch tomorrow anyway. It seems silly you going home now, and Sonny is having a blast with Vernon."

"Blimey, take a breath now and then, sis." Sam laughed. "If you're sure? We'd love to. I need to take Sonny for his evening walk first, always best to stick with his routine when possible."

"Deal. If you tell me what you fancy food wise, we can order while you're out."

"I don't know. Anything with chicken, you choose for me." She dipped a hand into her handbag and pulled out her purse.

"How dare you? Don't be so insulting, this one is on me."

"I can pay my way, sis."

"I know but I invited you to stay, so I'm willing to foot the bill."

"You're too kind. Thank you. I'll repay the favour in a couple of weeks, maybe take you both out for a meal once Vernon has recovered."

"That'll be lovely. All right, what about sweet and sour chicken, we could all share the dishes, if that's all right with you?"

"Sounds great. Can you let Sonny out for me so I won't have to take my shoes off only to put them on again?"

Sonny was whining at the sound of her voice.

"He's missed you, even though Vernon has tired him out this afternoon. He was curled up on the sofa when I got back." Her sister cringed at the admission.

"You two spoil him."

The ginger Exocet came tearing out of the lounge and almost knocked Sam over. His whining became high-pitched, so she got down on her haunches and snuggled into his fur. Unexpected tears bulged and ran down her cheeks. "What have I done to you, Sonny? Please forgive me for putting you through this."

"Hey, what's all this? You can't blame yourself for your husband walking out on you. And don't for one second think that Sonny is upset by the situation. He's fine, you have my word on that. Yes, he's missed you today, but I'm sure that's normal."

Sam stood and wandered into Crystal's outstretched arms. "I feel so guilty palming him off on to other people, it's irresponsible of me to do it as a dog owner."

"It's not at all. Being irresponsible would be leaving Sonny to fend for himself all day. You haven't done that, and if I know you as well as I do, you would never entertain doing such a thing to the little guy. Come on, brush those tears away, you've done nothing wrong, sweetheart."

"But how can you say that? I've driven Chris away—he must really hate me, not once has he bothered to call me to let me know where he's staying or to tell me he's all right. Why? Does he truly hate me that much?"

"Who knows what's going through that daft head of his most of the time? He's always been a touch reserved in my opinion."

"I guess you're right." She collected Sonny's lead from the coatrack and attached it to his red collar. "Come on, munchkin, the walk will do us both good. Sorry for breaking down, Crystal, I'm tired, and it's been a hectic week."

"You don't have to apologise to me, love. Have a nice walk."

CHAPTER 9

"*M*iranda, wake up. It's all right. I'm here for you." Tim shook his sister. Her screams had brought him running into her room to make sure she was okay.

She stirred, tears evident on her cheeks as if she had been crying nonstop in her sleep throughout the night. "What? Oh God, make them go away, Tim."

"I'm doing my best. There's only one more we have to deal with now, love. Hang in there. Another few days, and it'll all be over."

Miranda kicked the quilt back and shot out of bed. She ran to the window and pulled back the curtains. "I can't do this, not any more. They're coming after me in my sleep. I'm scared shitless at night, too frightened to close my eyes. When I eventually drift off to sleep, they're there, threatening me. Telling me what they're going to do to me."

Tim raced across the room and slung an arm around her shoulders. "You need to let it go, hon. We're doing all of this for the greater good. You suffered at the hands of these men, please, don't lose sight of how much they degraded you and what they put you through. You're a much stronger person now. Look at you. You've been enjoying punishing these men, haven't you?"

"I thought so, at the time… but the nightmares… all that blood, I can hear their screams and I just can't get it out of my head. The nightmares are destroying me. We shouldn't have taken our revenge in this way. I will never be the same again. Not after all of this. We can't kill anyone else, I won't allow it. I can't live with the guilt, not now, nor in the future. You have no idea what is going on in my head."

Tim took a step back. "Then tell me. What's going on up there?"

"If I could tell you, don't you think I would have done it before this? My life has been one massive nightmare over the years. I'm at the end of my tether. I've tried to end it all before, and I'm in danger of doing it again. I have the same desires running through my veins. I can't count the times I've lain there awake at night, reliving the pain and torture these men have put me through. When will it end? What will it take for all this to stop?" She jabbed her forehead with her finger.

"We can get you the professional help you need, love. We'll go private if we have to. The NHS is still snowed under with the pandemic, but it doesn't matter. We've got the money behind us. Seeing a professional will sort you out, I'm sure it will."

Miranda crossed her bedroom again to sit on the bed. She held her head in her hands. Tim was unsure what to do next, should he go to her or leave her alone?

Instead, he searched the internet via his phone for a local psychiatrist. Although it was Sunday, he rang the numbers; none of them had out-of-office hours. He left a message on a couple of the answerphones for someone to get back to him regarding an urgent appointment. "There, I've taken the first step for you."

Miranda glanced up. Her chin wobbled, and fresh tears appeared. "What would I do without you? Your kindness knows no bounds. You truly are my guardian angel."

"Nonsense. I do it because I love you. All of this was done in the same vein. We must stick together and try to get you back on track. To me, you're still guilty of letting the bastards bring you down. Don't allow that to happen, Miranda. Please. Don't you want to be well again?"

Her head jutted forward, and she ran her tongue across her dry lips. "Of course I do. I'd love nothing more than to have peace and serenity in my life. How am I supposed to obtain that if we continue to kill them? All this has been wrong, we should never have gone down this route. My nightmares are the worst they've ever been; I have to put that down to our willingness to kill these men. We're in the wrong, you have to admit it."

He blew out a breath that puffed out his cheeks and ran a hand through his hair. "I thought I was doing what was right for you. If you want us to stop then that's what we'll do. But you also need to see a psychiatrist. I'm sorry I've pushed you to the edge with the plan we put into place."

"Your plan. I just went along with your dream. I had my doubts this would work and I've been proved right. I want my life back. I want to sleep. At least before all this began, I was getting around three hours restful sleep every night. Now, all I do is constantly fend off the demons in my nightmares. There's blood everywhere. Blood and violence. I don't want that, Tim. All I want is what little sanity I have left to be preserved. I'll see a psychiatrist, but don't hold out much hope of them helping me. If it was up to me, I'd end it all tomorrow."

"Don't say that. Don't you love me?"

Miranda grasped his hand and kissed the back of it. "More than you'll ever know. But love won't mend my broken mind. I've lived with these dark thoughts for years. I can't go on. It's not natural to be so depressed all the time."

I thought she'd enjoyed killing Peter. Why the change of heart? I'm confused. "Seeing the doctor will ease your burden, love. I'm sure it will. Don't give up just yet. Hey, where the fuck would I be without you to care for?"

"Better off. You could settle down with a decent woman, have the family you've always craved, without me dragging you down with me. I'm rotten to the core, always have been."

He grabbed the tops of her arms and shook her a little. "Don't ever put yourself down like that. You're a wonderful, giving person, who has been destroyed by men taking advantage of your generous, loving nature."

She swallowed and rested her head against his shoulder. "I want all this to end."

She wants what to end? The killings or her life? The more she breaks down the harder it is for me to know what to do for the best. I only want to do what's right for her.

His arms crept around her in a vice-like grip. She was where she should be, in the safety of his embrace. Sod all the other men out there. He could give her all the love she needed, there was no need for her to search for it elsewhere. He had everything covered.

CHAPTER 10

*S*am had a leisurely lie-in on the Sunday, despite feeling guilty about not going into work. She helped Crystal chop and prepare the vegetables for the roast dinner, and then her sister ordered her to take a stroll around the park, making the most of the beautiful spring day.

"Come on, Sonny, let's go." She placed Sonny in the back of the car and drove to her usual park, not really knowing if there were any safe, dog-friendly parks close to Crystal's house.

Her gaze was drawn to the small bridge at the end where she had shared a kiss with Rhys. She had missed not seeing him every day. The last she had heard was his practice was doing exceptionally well and his days were getting considerably longer. Which had come as a complete surprise to him. He'd confided in Sam that he was that busy that he was now on the lookout for another psychiatrist to join him, part-time initially, although he predicted the rate his business was growing, the position would turn into a full-time appointment soon enough.

Sonny bolted towards the large oak tree close to the bridge. Sam trotted along the winding path, doing her best to keep up.

"Hey, I'm trying to keep up with you, and here you are, doing your best to get away from me," a voice she recognised came from behind, stopping her in her tracks.

It's him! Shit! Play it cool. Turning with a smile fixed in place, she said, "Hi, stranger. How have you been?"

"How to make a man feel bad. I'm sorry, I kept meaning to call you, but one thing led to another, and I found myself slotting in evening appointments, and before I knew it, I was finishing at the office and going home straight to bed."

"You don't have to make excuses to me, it's not like we're marr…" She bit down on her tongue.

He took a step towards her and placed a hand on her cheek. "I've been desperate to see you. How are things?"

"The same. Chris is still missing. To be honest, I'm past caring about him, if he can't be bothered to contact me then why should I waste my time worrying about him? He made his decision the day he walked out of my house."

Rhys shook his head. "That's disgusting! How can he treat you like this?"

"Easily, he's proven that already. I'm done with him. From this day forward, I'm considering myself young, free and single."

"Quite right, too. Have you eaten?"

"Sorry, not yet, but I'm expected at my sister's house for dinner. You could always come with me." The words escaped her mouth before she had a chance to stop them.

"I think your family might have something to say about that, but thank you for the offer. We'll catch up soon, I'm sure."

"But when?" There I go again. What's wrong with me? I sound desperate! What am I saying? I am desperate to see him.

155

"Let me get work organised and running like a well-oiled machine and then I'll be all yours." He turned towards the trees and called for his dog. "Benji, come on, boy, we have to go now."

"But..." The one word lingered in the air like a threat between them.

"Never any buts. It's work, Sam, I promise. I have every intention of seeing you regularly once my work life is stable. I've never been one to mess with someone's head, despite what you may have heard about shrinks." He laughed.

Her cheeks warmed under his intense gaze. Seconds later and the spell was broken between them when Benji's panting could be heard. Sam glanced down to find the Labrador obediently sitting on the grass, staring up at his dad. She peered over her shoulder to see where Sonny was. He was oblivious to what was going on, scouring the hedgerow and looking for signs of bunnies. "You've got my number."

"I have. Bear with me. It's a demanding time. I'm not ignoring you intentionally, I would never do that to you. The last thing you want to hear on a date is me going on about how busy work is."

He mentioned the D word. Oh God! Act cool. "It's fine, I promise. Don't think anything more of it. Ring me when you can and we'll try to arrange something. I understand where you're coming from, I worked six days myself last week, so you're definitely not alone."

"That can only mean you've been dealing with some seriously bad crimes. Have you?"

"You're good. And yes, we think we have a couple of serial killers on the loose, one male and one female."

He frowned. "Are we talking about two different serial killers or a double act?" Rhys took a swift look at his watch. "Sorry, I have to go. I've squeezed in a new patient who is desperate for my help, she'll be arriving at my office in ten minutes. I'll be cutting it fine if I don't go now."

"Go. We'll chat soon."

Rhys pecked her on the cheek and jogged out of the park. She watched on while he took another piece of her heart with him.

I'm acting like a teenage girl with a severe crush. "Sonny, come on, boy, where are you?"

"If you're looking for a cockapoo, I saw him shoot through the hedge. You really should keep a closer eye on your dog," an elderly woman walking a Jack Russell terrier chastised.

Sam chose to ignore the woman and not get involved in an argument. How could she when she knew the woman was right? She ran back to the spot she'd last seen him, frantically calling his name. "Sonny, here, Sonny. Look what Mummy has for you." She rattled the treat bag she'd had the sense to fetch with her, and miraculously, Sonny shoved his head through the hedge. "Sonny, come on, you can make it."

He whimpered and disappeared again. She rattled the bag of treats, and this time he leapt through the small opening and sat beside her begging for nibbles. Sam attached the leash, gave him a beef chew and marched back to the car. "You'll be the bloody death of me one of these days."

THE REST of the afternoon was spent in excellent company. Her sister and brother-in-law made sure she laughed until her sides hurt with different anecdotes about Vernon's footballing career, specifically what bizarre antics he got up to on the training ground each day with some of the other footballers. Plus, Crystal entertained them with stories about the type of questions she got asked by brides and their mothers. It amazed her how silly some people could be.

"Right, well, it's time I was going, as much as I hate to leave. You've been amazing. This weekend has been just what I needed to put my life back into perspective once more. I can't thank you both enough for being there for me."

Crystal sat forward on the sofa next to her and placed a hand over hers. "We're always here for you, Sam, don't ever think you're alone on this journey. Just give us a call if, and when, you want to stay with us. We've got an open house where you and Sonny are concerned."

Sonny was receiving some extra fuss from Vernon. It pleased her to see her dog so happy. "Sonny is well and truly at home here."

"I have a suggestion if you're up for it?" Vernon said.

"What's that?" Sam's gaze drifted between Crystal and Vernon.

"Why don't I look after Sonny during the day for the next couple of weeks while I'm off work? I should be up on my feet again from Wednesday. I'm bound to be ordered to get more exercise, I can start taking him for walks to help regain my fitness."

"I can't ask you to do that for me."

"You're not, I'm volunteering. Sam, it's what families are for, I'm sure you'd do the same for us if the tables were turned," Vernon insisted.

Sam was momentarily lost for words by the kind gesture. "I don't know what to say."

"*Yes* would be coming out of my mouth right now." Crystal nudged Sam's leg and laughed.

"Yes, yes, yes. How's that? Seriously, knowing that Sonny will be looked after so well in my absence is a huge relief to me."

"Will your neighbour be okay about the arrangement?" Crystal asked.

"I'm sure. I've felt uncomfortable putting on Doreen this

week. I know she says she doesn't mind, but I think she's just being kind. If you're sure it's not going to be too much of an inconvenience for you, Vernon?"

"Take my word on it, it's not. I'm looking forward to having Sonny keep me company during the day. When you're forced to stay at home, you feel like the walls are closing in on you, I can assure you. It'll be therapeutic having him around."

"That's a deal then. I can drop him off every day on my way into work. I'll bring his food with me." She wagged her finger. "That doesn't mean you can sit there all day feeding him treats."

Vernon slapped a hand over his chest and with the other he ruffled Sonny's head. "As if I would dream of doing that, Sonny."

Sonny angled his head backwards to view Vernon, and they all laughed.

"All right then, I'd love to take you up on the offer. I'll drop him off at eight-thirty in the morning, if that's all right with you? Will you be up?"

"Cheeky mare, of course I'll be up. I have a date with Lorraine every morning around that time."

Sam's brow furrowed, and she glanced at her sister for clarification. "Lorraine Kelly on ITV. I get the lowdown on what's going on in the fashion world every evening over dinner."

"That's too funny for words." Sam rose to her feet. "Again, you've both saved my life. I can't thank you enough for all you do for me. Don't ever hesitate to give me a shout if ever you need me to repay the favour."

"Ah, now you mention it, I've got this drawer full of parking tickets in the office."

Sam shook her head. "You're on your own there, Vernon, sorry."

He tutted and smiled. "I'm only joshing with you."

Sam kissed them both and began packing the car. She decided to leave most of Sonny's possessions behind, knowing she had duplicates of everything back at the house, except for his bed. Sonny usually slept with her anyway.

"Right, come on, munchkin, it's time for us to go. Say goodbye to Uncle Vernon and Auntie Crystal."

Sonny licked them both goodbye and trotted to the front door.

"He's such an intelligent dog," Crystal admired in the hallway.

"Sometimes. He's wonderful, my world would be a much duller place without him."

"He's a credit to you. Are you going to be all right, Sam?"

"Of course. I have a great family behind me. I don't like to burden Mum and Dad with my problems, but having you and Vernon by my side going forward is going to be a massive help."

"You'll meet someone worthy of your love soon, I'm sure."

Sam flustered and dropped Sonny's lead.

Crystal clutched her arm. "It's already happened, hasn't it? Is this the fella at the park you told us about?"

"Umm... the truth is, I don't know. He's setting up a new business right now, and I've barely seen him, although I did bump into him at the park earlier."

Crystal bashed a fist against her thigh. "I knew something had happened while you were out, you seemed a little distant for about half an hour upon your return. Have you fallen for him?"

Sam closed her eyes and nodded. "I think so," she whispered.

"Good for you. Hey, why the hesitation? You're single, your husband doesn't give a shit, that much is bloody obvious. My advice would be to go for it."

"I don't know. There's something I can't put my finger on, holding me back. I'd rather take things slowly for now, it's not like I know him well, not really."

"You know the answer to that, get to know him pronto, before someone else beats you to it. You can't afford to miss an opportunity when it lands on your plate, love, not at your age."

Sam gasped. "Hark at you. For your information, I'm thirty-two not fifty-two."

Crystal dismissed her claim with a flap of her hand. "Whatever, you know what I mean."

"Yeah, I do. But what if Chris comes swanning back into my life, what then?"

"I know what I would do. Knee him in the balls and tell him to sod off."

"You wouldn't dare?"

Her sister gave her a determined look. "Try me."

"I love you so much." Sam hugged her. "I'll get through this. Thanks for always being there for me."

"Ditto. Now go before we both end up in tears. And don't worry about Sonny during the day, Vernon will look after him well."

"I have no doubts about it. Thanks again. You're the best sister a girl could ever hope to have." She left the house with Sonny and drove home.

Sonny ran ahead of her once she'd slipped off his lead. She followed him up the hallway and into the kitchen and shuddered. There was a chill in the air, so she flicked the heating to Manual and made a note to turn it off again in an hour when the house had warmed through. After refreshing the water in Sonny's bowl, Sam wandered upstairs. The house appeared to be even colder up there. Her bedroom felt like the inside of a freezer, and it wasn't until she went into the en suite that she realised why—she'd left the window open. Not that she remembered doing it. *Did I? I could have sworn I closed it after having my shower yesterday.* She scanned the room, and everything seemed in place. She opened the wardrobe and stood back. Her side was still full, but Chris's was completely empty.

He's been here! He must have left the window open, why? Out of spite? Why come back here after all this time? Has he been watching the house? Was his trip intentional? Did he know I wouldn't be here?

Sam ran back downstairs to check what else he'd taken. There were some personal things missing from the lounge— his laptop and a few trophies he'd collected for various sports over the years. It was then that her nose twitched and she realised his aftershave was lingering throughout the house. He must have been here recently. There was only one thing for it, she would nip next door and ask Doreen if she'd seen him.

"I'll be right back, Sonny." Taking her keys with her, she strode up the path and into her neighbour's garden.

Doreen answered the door quickly. "Hello, Sam. How are you, dear?"

"I'm fine, Doreen. I've just come back from spending the weekend with my sister and her husband to find that Chris has been in the house. Did you see him?"

Doreen glanced over Sam's shoulder and heaved out a sigh. "Silly me, I knew I recognised the car. I didn't think anything of it at the time, not until you just mentioned it. I take it he didn't hang around to speak with you?"

"No. He took some stuff with him, left a window open and vanished."

"How odd. I'm sorry, Sam, if you ask me, he seems intent on messing with your head."

"I was thinking the same. Never mind. Sorry to disturb you."

"Don't be. Will Sonny be joining me this week?"

Sam cringed. "Ah, sorry, no. My brother-in-law has volunteered to look after him, if that's okay with you?"

"You don't have to ask for my blessing. As long as Sonny is being cared for properly, my offer still stands, you know that."

"Thanks so much, Doreen. I'll catch up with you during the week."

"Take care, Samantha."

The first thing Sam did once her front door was shut was to drop the latch. There was no way Chris was coming back in the house without her knowing it tonight, but where did that leave her during the week while she was stuck at work? She scrolled through her phone for a local locksmith and left a message to one who was based just up the road. Maybe Doreen would oversee the job for her if he had a vacant slot during the week.

How has it come to this? Why wouldn't he come to the house while I was here? Right, Chris, up until now I was prepared to let things slide, but that's about to change after this. You'd better watch out, matey, you won't know what's hit you when my solicitor gets hold of you. If I can find you, that is!

CHAPTER 11

*B*ob was driving along the main road into work, tapping his fingers and playing the air guitar at the traffic lights, listening to Rock FM, when out of the corner of his eye he saw someone he recognised. *What the fuck is Chris doing here?* He indicated and drew into a parking space and turned in his seat to watch. Chris had come out of a detached house. There was a blonde wearing a silky dressing gown standing at the front door. She was grinning like a Cheshire cat, waving and blowing kisses at him. *Boy, oh boy. You're in trouble now, you dipshit!*

He watched Chris's reaction. He seemed okay with all the attention. Bob quickly came to the conclusion this woman wasn't just one of Chris's customers, there was something far more going on between them. *Fuck, how the heck am I going to tell Sam? Should I tell her? What if I'm wrong?* He continued to watch as Chris drew away from the house and papped his horn at the sexy woman. Bob waited until Chris passed him and then pulled out behind him. At the next set of traffic lights, Bob unhitched his seatbelt and exited the car. He tapped on Chris's window.

Chris lowered it, shocked to see him. "Hello, Bob, how are you? Long time no see, mate."

"*Mate*? I'm not your frigging mate. I saw you back there. What was that all about?"

"What did I miss? What are you talking about?"

"You and Mrs Sex on Legs? And don't try and pull the wool over my eyes either."

Chris glanced ahead of him and swallowed loudly. "I've got to go, the lights have changed."

Horns blasted behind them. "Either you pull over in the next lay-by or…"

Chris sped away, and Bob ran back to the car. He gave the finger to the impatient drivers behind him and put his foot down. Chris drove another half a mile and then indicated into the lay-by up ahead. Bob shot out of the car and slipped into the passenger seat beside Chris.

"So? Now you've had time to contemplate my question, I want an answer, and don't bother lying to me. I'm a savvy detective for a reason and I know when my eyes are deceiving or not."

Chris leaned forward and rested his head on the steering wheel. "I'm sorry."

"Too right you fucking are, now that you've been caught out. What the fuck are you playing at? Treating Sam like this, are you insane?"

"We're over. Surely she's told you that."

"She thinks you're on a break, wait until she knows the truth. Go on, tell me, how long has this sleazy affair been going on?"

Chris sat up and faced him. "It's not a sleazy or sordid affair, Donna and I love each other."

Bob covered his face with his hands. They slipped back down to his lap in slow motion, giving him time to think. "What the fuck are you on about? You've got a wife, you can't go around falling in love with slappers when the fancy takes you."

"Don't call her that. She's a loving woman who I adore."

"Put yourself in my position. If you saw me coming out of a bird's house and you knew I was married, what the fuck would you be calling the other woman?" Bob growled. "Don't bother answering. Jesus, Sam doesn't deserve to be treated this way. You've been a bastard to her for years, and now this."

"I dispute that. Don't judge me just by what you've heard from her mouth. Our marriage was rock-solid until we bought that house."

"A doer-upper that you wrecked without her permission, I seem to recall."

"If I hadn't made the first move, the house would never get renovated."

"You put her in debt and then you thought 'I know what, I'll go screw around a little, teach her a lesson'. Am I right? Don't answer that, it's written all over your face. You dickhead, how could you? She's been out of her mind most days because you haven't been in touch, and all the time you're screwing sex on legs back there. And no, that's not me giving you a pat on the back for hooking a stunning bird with no morals. Does she know? About Sam?" His gaze dropped to Chris's left hand. There was no wedding ring in sight.

"No. She thinks I'm single."

"Way to go, Chris. So that's two birds you've been lying to. For how long?"

Chris wiped a hand around his face. "A couple of months."

"I should get you out of this car and give you a fucking good hiding for what you've put Sam through. You're scum, worse than fucking pond life. You're a disrespecting individual who needs to go ten rounds in a ring with a champion boxer. Maybe that would knock some sense into you."

Chris was silent for a few seconds before he finally found his voice. "Don't give me that bullshit. If you had the green light, you'd get your leg over, given the chance."

Bob struck out, grasped Chris around the neck and raised his fist.

"I swear to God, I'll do you for assault if you strike me," Chris said nervously.

Bob thrust him away and let out a growl that hurt his throat. "You know what, I can't be bothered. You'd better keep looking over your shoulder, scumbag, because I'm going to be gunning for you until you have the guts to get in touch with Sam and tell her what depths you've sunk to."

"You can't force me."

"No, you're right, I can't. But I'm warning you, don't take me for a fool, mate, not if you want to continue trading and to live a free life." He clicked his finger and thumb together. "I could stitch you up with any number of crimes, just like that, and you wouldn't know what hit you, arsehole."

"Why am I not surprised to hear you say that? If you're trying to scare me, it ain't working. Sam and I were over long ago, she'd be the first to admit it."

"You're missing the point, fuckhead, you need to have the balls to tell her to her face rather than screw another bitch behind her back. A real man would choose to do it that way round. What am I saying? You're not a real man, are you?"

"Screw you! You're talking out of your arse as usual. Like you know what it's like living with a woman who puts her job before her relationship."

"I do, take it from me, Sam ain't like that, and if you truly believe she does that then you're not worth her crying over. You think she's happy about you walking out on her? I may

167

be speaking out of turn, but take my word for it, she's been devastated these last couple of weeks."

"If she's been so cut up about it then why did she spend the weekend away with someone?"

Bob shook his head, confused. "What are you talking about? She's done nothing of the sort. For a start she was with me on Saturday, at work, and the rest of the weekend she spent at Crystal's place. So again, there you have it, another case of you getting your facts wrong."

Chris sighed. "I ain't going to apologise, my marriage was a mess. It's about time we realised we weren't suited."

"So why didn't you have the balls to sit down and discuss it with her instead of just walking out and leaving her hanging? It's a good job she's got a strong will."

"Too strong at times," Chris bit back. "This is no concern of yours. So back off and leave us to it."

"Had I not seen you coming out of that slapper's house, I would have agreed with you, your marriage shouldn't be any concern of mine. The trouble is, I've seen you with my own eyes, and you've just admitted that you've been shagging that bitch for months. I'm not the type to walk away and let a colleague down."

"Stop calling her names. She's nothing like you envisage."

Bob raised an eyebrow. "You'll be telling me next the Pope isn't Catholic. Trying to talk yourself out of the situation is only going to make things a hundred times worse."

"I'm doing nothing of the sort. I've admitted it, haven't I?"

"To me, maybe. What you need to do is have the guts to tell Sam what's going on. You know she calls the mortuary every day to see if you're a new arrival, don't you?" Bob knew he was talking bullshit, but the way Chris went green around the gills had a satisfying effect.

"She doesn't?"

"Yep. Tell me, what else is she supposed to do if you can't be fucking arsed to get in touch?"

"I never thought."

"Why would you give her a second thought if you're cosied up with Sexy Legs 2022? You know what, Chris? You're a hell of a guy. Let's just say I'm glad you're no friend of mine. I think it's contemptible the way you've treated Sam and I'm not just saying it because she happens to be my boss either. Men like you give the rest of us a bad rep."

"What can I say? I've apologised. I can't turn the clock back."

"No, you're right, you can't, but what you can do is make amends and call your damn wife."

"I will. Eventually."

Bob leaned in closer, his gaze boring into Chris's. "You'll do it now, within the next few days. Don't forget I know where you're staying. I'll have no hesitation showing up at your little love nest and telling Sexy Legs what her latest beau has been up to."

"I said I'll do it."

Bob clutched the handle on the door and leaned into Chris again. "I'm glad we had a chance to have this little chat and that I was able to put my point across. Now do the right thing. You've got twenty-four hours, gutless wonder."

"Whatever," Chris mumbled.

Bob left the van and deliberately slammed the door behind him. Chris revved the engine and roared off before Bob had even reached his own car. *Bastard! I hope that woman ends up married and her husband teaches you a lesson.*

He continued his journey to the station, pondering an excruciating dilemma—whether to tell Sam or not.

"Are you deaf?"

"What?" Bob said.

Sam trotted to catch up with her partner. "I must have called you dozens of times and you totally blanked me. Is that any way to treat your commanding officer?"

"Sorry, I've got things on my mind."

"No shit, Sherlock. Anything you want to share?"

"Not really. Maybe in a day or so."

Sam frowned and tilted her head. "A problem shared and all that."

"You have enough on your plate. How was the rest of your weekend?"

"I suppose you could call it mixed."

"Meaning?"

"I'll tell you inside." Sam shuddered and pulled up her collar to ward off the sharp breeze.

"Over a coffee, no doubt."

"How did you guess?"

They entered the main entrance.

"Morning, ma'am, Bob," Nick, the desk sergeant, welcomed them.

"Morning, Nick. Anything to report this morning?"

"All clear so far. I hear you had a busy weekend. I was just catching up on the paperwork."

"Let's put it this way, it was eventful," Sam replied with a weary smile.

"Give me a shout if you need my lads to lend a hand with anything, what with you being snowed under with three separate cases to deal with now."

"Don't worry, I have every intention of doing that, Nick." She punched in her code, and the security door clicked open. Halfway up the stairs, she asked, "Does your mood reflect what went on over the weekend, you know, is there trouble at home again? Did Abigail batter your credit card at the shops?"

"No, nothing to do with that, I promise. In fact, I got off lightly this time. I warned her before she went, if she wants a holiday abroad this year, we'd need to watch what we spend over the next few months."

"Ah, the thought of relaxing on a white sandy beach on distant shores worked wonders then. Good to hear. That reminds me, I need to take a look at the holiday schedule, book a couple of weeks away at a cottage for me and Sonny."

"Sounds great. Where do you fancy going?"

"I thought we'd head up to Scotland, maybe around Loch Ness, that area. Have you ever ventured up that far?"

"No, never. I've heard it's magical, though."

"Me, too."

Sam pushed through the door to the incident room to find most of her team already at their desks. "Morning, all. I hope you had a good weekend. Let me get my coat off and whizz through the post and then I'll bring you up to date with the developments. Yes, please, Bob, milk with one sugar."

Her partner rolled his eyes.

He seems different today, why? Is he tired? Aren't we all? Or is he going through more problems at home, even though he's just denied it? I'll wheedle the information out of him, eventually.

She groaned at the amount of post littering her desk.

"Bloody hell, it's getting worse than ever. I don't envy you wading through that lot today."

She peered over her shoulder at her partner and slipped off her coat. "Feel free to suggest we swap jobs for the day."

Bob's mouth twisted. "Nope, that's not going to happen. I'll leave you to it and hope the caffeine kicks in soon to help ease you through it."

"You're too kind. I'll give it a quick scan and be out soon. Can you chase up the camera footage? We're going to need that more than ever after the latest murder."

"I'm on it. I'll leave you to this lot."

"Thanks, Bob." Sam sat behind her desk and opened her first letter. She took several sips of coffee to help with the onerous task.

Ten minutes later, her forefinger borderline bruised by the experience, she completed her chore and headed back into the incident room with the remains of her coffee. "Okay, as you will have noticed, I've added a third name to the board. Have you filled the team in or not, Bob? I wouldn't want to repeat myself."

He held his arms out. "I haven't had a chance."

"Right. Here we go then. Saturday morning, I was requested to join the pathologist and his team at The Flying Horse. The scene was gruesome, one of the worst I've witnessed during my long career. The landlord of the pub, Peter Richmond, was found in his cellar, tortured to death. Several wounds which had been caused by a couple of broken bottles. The bottles are being examined for possible DNA—there were fingerprints found on the necks."

"Kind of sloppy, boss," Claire suggested.

"I agree. There's more. We also found numerous foot-prints on the blood-spattered floor of the cellar. Careless or intentional? Bob and I have come to the conclusion that it's the latter and believe the killers—yes, there were two of them, I'll come to that in a moment—well, we believe the killers are toying with us. We're aware it happens, maybe it hasn't been as evident in previous cases as it is with this one, but that's our perception. What we need to find out is why."

Suzanna raised her hand. "Does this mean we're going to be expected to work on all three cases now, boss?"

Sam raised her hand. "I'm coming to that. Bob, do you have the footage of the two suspects from the pub to hand?"

He nodded and angled the remote control at the

widescreen TV behind Sam. The screen flickered to life, and Bob played the disc Sam had collected from the pub.

"As you can see, there is no one else left in the pub except these two, a man and a woman."

"Looks like they're wearing disguises," Claire offered.

"That's our assumption as well. If Bob can fast forward the disc for me to where the two suspects leave the pub." Sam paused while Bob carried out her instructions. "And here, both the suspects are covered in the man's blood."

"Wow, so she's as much to blame as he is," Liam piped up.

"It seems that way," Sam confirmed.

"Unless she tried to help the victim," Claire said, ever the practical member of the team.

"Something to consider for sure. The cameras outside the pub failed to highlight their vehicle, so Bob and I went back to the crime scene on Saturday afternoon and… can you bring up the next clip, Bob?"

The screen split into two; on the right-hand side was the image of the light-coloured Peugeot leaving the pub car park.

"And here, the car is easily identifiable as being theirs. What we need to do is trace the route it took, hopefully that will lead us to the suspects. Providing they haven't dumped the car by then."

"Have you run the plate through the system?" Alex asked.

"We did. The car was registered to someone in Wales. Bob rang the owner; he sold the car a few weeks ago to a couple matching the suspects' description, partially; by that I mean the man sold the car to a man and woman. It has to be them. Now, after sifting through the evidence from all three crimes, rightly or wrongly, Bob and I reckon that at least two, maybe all three, of the crimes are connected."

A sea of confused faces stared back at her.

Sam continued, "All right, let me run through how we've come to that conclusion, although we're waiting on forensics to come back to us on certain aspects. Case one, that of Brian Coltman. He was seen drinking with a young man by the name of Ian who escorted him back to his boat. The man left, only for the killer to arrive, what? Ten minutes later? Now some may class that as a coincidence, but after careful consideration, we believe differently. I've asked the pathologist to compare the fingerprints found at the last scene to any found on board the boat. Alex, what I want you to do is analyse the footage from both scenes—pay particular attention to the height of the suspect/known killer from the first case, see if they can possibly be the same person."

"I'll see what I can do, boss. What about the second case?"

"I'm coming to that. What do we know about the second case? We know that the victim, Ed Abbott, was instructed to pick up a female punter and drop her off near The Royal Oak in Seaton. Could the suspect at the third murder scene be the same person?"

"How are we going to figure that out, boss? We've got nothing so far on the woman," Claire stated.

"I know. Again, we're going to be relying on forensics to come up with the goods."

"Or CCTV footage," Bob added.

"I was just about to say the same. We're going to need to focus all our efforts, or most of them, on nailing that footage. All we have at present from the second scene is a tyre track— could that be traced back to the Peugeot? Again, we're not likely to get the results back yet, not for a few days. So, there we have it, folks. Yes, we're lumping all three cases together unless we come across evidence indicating we shouldn't. Let's concentrate on the footage that Bob is doing his best to obtain and see where that leads us."

"What about using a facial recognition expert?" Alex suggested.

"Yes, I already have that in mind. Let's piece together everything we have so far and go from there. If we can trace any other possible footage, we'll analyse it and see if someone over at forensics can corroborate our line of thinking."

"All we need then is to find the names of the suspects. Easy, right?" Bob tutted.

She grinned. "I'll leave you to oversee things out here while I crack on with the dreary part of the job I despise."

"Shout if you need a hand."

"I will, don't worry." Sam collected another coffee from the drinks' station and returned to her office. She tried to concentrate on the dreary paperwork but found herself drifting off as Rhys's image entered her mind. Eventually, with her attention declining, she took the plunge and rang his office.

"Hello there. Is it possible to speak with Rhys…?" She paused, suddenly realising she couldn't remember his surname. She hunted through her handbag, trying to trace the card he'd given her. "Ah, yes, here it is, Rhys Wilkins, sorry, Doctor Wilkins." Sam kicked herself for letting her nerves get the better of her.

"I knew who you meant, we've only got one Rhys here." The receptionist giggled. "He's between patients at the moment, who shall I say is calling?"

"Thanks, it's Detective Inspector Sam Cobbs."

"Oh, I see. Hold the line, please."

Sam picked up her pen and tapped it against her lips. *Am I doing the right thing, calling him like this?*

"I'm putting you through now," the secretary said.

"Sam, is that you?"

Her stomach clenched at the sensual timbre in his voice. "Yes, I'm so sorry to disturb you."

"You're not. I'm between patients. What can I do for you?

Is it official? Only you gave your full rank and name to my secretary, so I thought it must be."

"Possibly. No, I'm just teasing. Cards on the table, I can't stop thinking about you. There, I've said it."

"You've blown your cover at last. That makes two of us."

Relief flooded through her like a larger-than-life tidal wave. "What do you propose we do about our situation then?" she asked, wincing as the words tumbled out with a life of their own.

"Well, I could suggest dinner, but my schedule is pretty full-on again this week. Let me see if I can tweak things a little, hang on a sec."

She continued to tap the pen along to the words of Ed Sheeran's song 'Perfect' rattling through her mind.

Rhys blew out a breath. "All right, this is the best I can do at short notice. I've got a new patient booked in for tomorrow evening at six, I'll be with her for around an hour. What if we arrange to meet up at seven-thirty? Bearing in mind that I won't be able to go home and change before dinner."

"Sounds fabulous to me. It'll give me time to walk Sonny when I get home. Where shall we go?"

"What if you come to the office? I can give you the guided tour and then we can set off on foot. You can either come in by taxi, if you fancy a drink, or leave your car in the car park at the rear and pick it up after dinner."

"I prefer the first option. I'm looking forward to seeing you."

"Our first date. It's been a long time coming, Sam."

"It has. I know I'm doing the right thing."

"Good. I've felt you have put the brakes on too much in the past. We need to see where this is all going to lead to."

A knock on the door interrupted the conversation. Bob poked his head into the room and lingered.

"See you tomorrow, Rhys. I've got to go." Her cheeks warmed under her partner's gaze.

He flung himself into the vacant chair opposite her. "A date?"

"Would it be so wrong of me if I said yes?"

Bob stared at his hands and picked at his nails.

"Bob, do you think I'm doing the wrong thing?"

He shrugged and continued to avoid eye contact. "What do I know?"

Sam tore a sheet of paper off her pad, screwed it up into a ball and threw it at him. "Don't just sit there, talk to me."

"About what? Infidelity?"

Sam bounced back in her chair. "What? Are you having a go at me? May I remind you that I'm not the one who walked out on my marriage, Chris is."

"I know, and no, you don't have to remind me." Her partner still refused to meet her eye.

"Bob. Tell me what's going through that mind of yours. I'm sensing I've done something majorly wrong in your eyes."

He placed a clenched fist against his head and banged it a few times. "It's not you per se, it's me."

"What is? You're not making sense."

"All right, you're forcing this out of me. I've been reluctant about telling you, hoping that waste-of-space husband of yours would save me the trouble."

Sam shot forward in her chair again and pointed at him. "You're going to be in serious trouble if you don't tell me what the fuck you're on about. Are you telling me you've seen Chris?"

He nodded and whispered, "Yes."

Furious due to the revelation, Sam slammed her hand on the desk to gain his attention. "Spill. Where and when?"

"On the way into work this morning. I pulled him over to have a chat."

"And? Bob, for fuck's sake, tell me what's going on. Why won't you look at me?"

"I can't."

"Why? What the hell do you have to feel guilty about?"

"I don't feel guilty, why should I?"

She sighed and shook her head. "You tell me. That's the way I'm reading your body language. Let me have it, now!"

He rolled his head back and linked his fingers on top. "I saw him coming out of a house."

"So he was on a callout... wait a minute, what time was this?"

"Around eight-thirtyish. He came out of a house and jumped into his van."

"Back up a second, I don't like the intonation in your voice when you said that."

His hands slipped off his head and cradled his face. He chewed on his bottom lip.

"Okay, let me fill in the blanks for you. You saw him with another woman, didn't you?"

"Yes. She was in a silky dressing gown, waving him off."

"I want to know everything, don't hold back."

"Don't shout at me, I'm not the one in the wrong here, he is."

"That wasn't my intention. I apologise. I thought we were mates?"

"Don't throw that one into the mix. We are. I'm doing my best to tell you. It's not pretty, Sam, bear with me."

"Stop trying to protect my feelings and give it to me straight, I can take it. You suspect he's slept with this woman, right?"

"Worse than that. He's moved in with her."

Sam shrugged. "Life's a bitch. I've moved on, and so has he, apparently."

"Think about it, Sam."

"Oh, my Lord, are you telling me he was shagging her behind my back?"

He applauded the dawning of the truth. "Yes. What a bastard, eh?"

"Shit! Why in God's name didn't he tell me?"

"I had a go at him, pointed out his failings in not telling you. He couldn't give a shit, Sam, I'm sorry."

"I kind of figured that out for myself. So he led me to believe that I was to blame for the breakdown of our marriage and all the time he was busy giving this other woman one behind my back. What a total…"

"Yeah, I let him have it, I can tell you. It was his reaction that pissed me off, he was so blasé about it."

"You know why that is, don't you?"

Bob frowned.

"You really think he would have walked if he didn't have anywhere else to go?" she said. "What's wrong with me? I should have realised he was having an affair. Let's face it, most men dabble at one time or another."

"Now wait just a minute. I haven't, you can't tar us all with the same brush."

She raised her hands. "I admit, it was disrespectful of me."

"Too bloody right. What are you going to do about it?"

"I'm pissed off he went back to the house yesterday when I was out. Good job I have someone hopefully getting back to me today about changing the locks. The sooner that's done the better in my opinion."

"I've got a friend in the business, want me to arrange it?"

"If you could."

Bob jumped out of his chair, but before he left the room, he turned and said, "I've been tearing myself to pieces since

179

we arrived. I wanted to tell you so much. I should have just come out and said it first thing."

"You've told me now. Don't ever feel you have to sit on something, Bob. I like to think we have an open and honest relationship, I'd hate to see that change."

"That's me told. I'm sorry, Sam."

"Let's get past this. The truth is out there now. I can finally get on with my life."

"Sounds like you're doing that anyway."

She smiled. "Go call your friend for me."

He exited the room, and she was left reeling from the information he'd divulged.

You utter toerag, Chris Cobbs. How dare you do this to me and think you can get away with it? I might not do anything to get my revenge but I'll make sure the solicitor takes you for everything, and more, as punishment.

WITH THE PAPERWORK all tied up in a neat bow, Sam returned to the incident room to see how the team were getting on. She stopped off to speak to Bob first.

Keeping his voice low, he told her, "Everything is sorted. Kevin is going round there later. I told him to knock on Doreen's to collect the key. Did I do the right thing?"

"You did. I appreciate it, Bob."

"Always welcome."

"Any news on the cameras?"

"Liam and I have been tracking the car through the town. We thought we were doing well, and then it reached the country lanes and vanished."

"Intentional?" she asked, disappointment pummelling her stomach.

"Possibly."

Sam took a moment to consider what to do next. "All

right, let's not beat ourselves up about this. Here's what I want you to do. Go through the footage again, together, and pick out any clear shots you can get of the two suspects."

"We can do that. Why?"

"I've decided there's only one thing for it, to call another press conference. This time I'll ask the public for their assistance. Someone, somewhere must know who these fuckers are and where they live."

Bob winced. "While I hear what you're saying, cautiously I'm going to ask, isn't that a bit dangerous? Couldn't they go to ground?"

"I think the opposite, it'll help flush them out. Maybe they'll make a big mistake and slip up without realising it."

"What, during their next kill?"

"Hopefully it won't come to that. I'm going to give Jackie a call, get it organised now."

"If that's what you think we should do."

"I do, but I'll need those pictures ASAP."

"In other words, crack on and don't hold the horses."

Sam smiled, collected another cup of coffee and returned to her office where she rang Jackie. "Hey, are you busy?"

"No more than usual. I hear you're up against it working three cases, though. How can I help?"

She gave Jackie the quick lowdown of what she needed. "Can you fit me in, maybe late afternoon? That'll give the boys plenty of time to source some decent images for us to present to the public."

"You can count on me. I'll do the necessary and give you a call back in about an hour."

"Sounds good to me, thanks, Jackie."

"Don't mention it. Speak soon."

No sooner had she ended the call than her phone rang again. "DI Sam Cobbs, how can I help?"

"Sam, it's Des Markham. I take it you're well. I have news for you."

"Hi, Des." She sat to attention, bracing herself for hopeful news. "Good or bad news?"

"Oh, I would definitely class this as good news. I've had every member of forensics working over the weekend to bring you these results."

"What? You shouldn't have done that, even I had Sunday off."

"That's your prerogative. I wanted to get this sorted for you. And I believe we've managed to get you the results you've been waiting for."

"That's great. Hit me with it."

"I can confirm that the same trace evidence was found at all three scenes, therefore, I have no hesitation in telling you that the cases are linked and we know who the suspects are. All you have to do is catch them."

Sam punched the air. "As we thought. Not sure why we didn't figure it out sooner."

"Logically, because there was nothing linking the crimes, now there is. I'll get my reports typed up this morning and sent over to you either later this afternoon or tomorrow first thing, if that's okay?"

"It sounds perfect to me. I can't thank you enough, Des. Will you pass on my gratitude to your team as well?"

"There's no need. The three cases were bugging the life out of us, too. So working over the weekend was beneficial to all of us, if you get my drift."

"I hear you. Oh, one last thing, if I may? The tyre tread, any word on that?"

"Ah, yes. We believe it belongs to a Peugeot if that helps."

"It certainly does. Thanks again, Des."

"A pleasure, as always. Now go get the bastards."

"My intentions are bubbling as we speak."

CHAPTER 12

Tim had hit the drink heavily the night before and was now hungover. He lifted his head gingerly to see what time it was. "Bloody hell, it's already eleven." He eased himself upright, and bile rose in his throat. "Shit! I'm going to puke. I need to get a fried breakfast down my neck, that'll steady the old stomach."

He ventured along the hallway to the bathroom and poked his head into his sister's room en route. No movement there. He continued his journey, did the necessary, only managing to hold on to the contents of his stomach by a thread, then he went to check on Miranda again to ask if she was game for a full English.

"Miranda. Miranda, are you awake? We're lazy buggers, it's gone eleven. I'm going to knock up some breakfast, are you up for having the works?"

There was no response. He walked heavy-footed into the room, doing his best to try and wake her. It was relatively dark because of the blackout curtains his sister had insisted they should buy. He opened the curtains and glanced down at her. "Come on, sleepyhead. What the fuck? No! Miranda, no!"

There was blood coming from her wrists, staining the cream lacy quilt cover. His mind was too foggy from soaking up last night's alcohol to function correctly. He paced back and forth a few times and then approached the bed. "Miranda, please, don't be dead. Wake up!"

With his head a touch clearer, he bent down beside her and felt for a pulse. "Thank God, she's alive. I need to get you to the hospital."

He shoved the quilt back and saw that she was wearing a pair of fleecy pyjamas. He tapped her face in the hope this would wake her. She stirred a little and groaned. He tapped some more.

"What? Where am I?"

"You're at home, but I'm taking you to the hospital."

"No. I don't want to go. Let me end it, Tim. I need to go now."

"I refuse to let you go. I'm not going to let you do this. I love you. I need you here with me. I'm sorry for letting you down. For putting you through this shit. I thought I was doing the right thing. I didn't realise it would send you over the edge, please, please forgive me. Don't leave me. I'll be nothing without you." His head banging the more he spoke, he rested it on her chest and gripped her arms.

She stroked his hair. "I can't do this any more. I don't want to live. You need to let me go."

He raised his head to look at her. "I can't, you're my life. If I let you go, I'd have to kill myself as well."

"No, you would go on without me. You're far stronger than I am, please let me go."

"I can't. I need to get you to the hospital. We've got an appointment with the psychiatrist tomorrow. He'll help you through this bad patch. I have faith in him, he sounds like the real deal, Miranda. You have to give this one last shot. The others didn't understand you. I'm sure this one will be different. Come on, we need to get you to the hospital. Shit, I'm not dressed, I need to throw some clothes on. Stay there, I'll be right back." He left her, ran back to his bedroom and grabbed the pile of dirty clothes in the corner. The movement made him sway. His head felt heavier by the second, but he knew if he didn't get her to the hospital what the likelihood of losing her would be. He ran back to the bedroom to find his sister drowsy.

She allowed him to sit her upright. Even though it felt like his head belonged to someone else, he forced himself to concentrate on the task in hand. Miranda was limp in his arms, she had no energy. He had to dig deep into his reserves to conjure up the strength to pull both of them to their feet.

"I can't go like this," she murmured, her head settled against his shoulder.

"You're going to have to. You're too weak, I need a doctor to see you right away." He lifted her into his arms and carried her downstairs, only stopping by the slim table in the hallway to pick up his car keys. He slammed the front door behind him and slipped Miranda into the passenger seat. He toyed with the idea of nipping back to grab her coat but instead reached into the back seat and snatched up the travel rug. He tucked it around her.

She smiled sleepily at him and whispered, "I love you."

He shut the door and ran around to the driver's seat and started the engine. The hospital was around twenty-five minutes away. He attached his seatbelt and eased into a gap in the traffic passing the house, for once grateful they lived on the main road into town. Every now and then he checked on his sister. She kept dozing all through the journey. Eventually, he managed to get to Accident and Emergency. He searched the central console for some change, parked close to the main entrance and swept Miranda up into his arms.

The receptionist's expression was one of concern. "Is she all right?"

"Does she look it? She's cut her wrists, I need her to be seen right away."

"Okay, let me get some details first."

"I don't have time for this, she's weak and has lost a lot of blood."

"You should have called for an ambulance, she could have been treated at the scene."

He glared at the young redhead and seethed. "Well, I didn't. I thought it would be better if I brought her here myself. Now are you going to get a doctor or not?"

"In a moment. I need her name and date of birth?"

"What the fuck?"

"Excuse me. There's no need to swear at me, all I'm trying to do is assist you, sir."

"Please, Tim, don't have a go at her. She's only doing her job," Miranda whispered.

"Miranda Wallace, tenth of February, nineteen eighty-nine."

"There, that wasn't difficult, was it? Take a seat, I'll pass her details on to the doctor in charge."

"How long is he likely to be? She's fading fast. I don't want to lose her."

"It depends on how busy he is. Take a seat."

Tim reluctantly set Miranda in one of the plastic chairs near the window and sat next to her, gripping her hand tightly. He stared back at the reception desk and noticed the small pool of blood on the floor where he had been standing, holding his dying sister.

Within seconds, a young male doctor came to collect them. "Miranda Wallace, I take it?"

"Yes. You have to help her. She's still losing a lot of blood."

"Do you want me to get a trolley or can you carry her through to triage?"

"I can carry her. We have to hurry, Doc. I'm not sure how long she has left."

"Okay. This way."

Tim carried his sister through the wide hallway to a cubicle at the end.

"I'll need to assess her first. I'll get the equipment."

"Please, hurry, Doc."

"Don't worry, she's in safe hands now." The doctor left the cubicle and returned wheeling a monitor a few minutes later. He was accompanied by a nurse.

"You're going to need to wait outside, sir," the nurse instructed Tim.

"I can't, she needs me."

"Tim, I'm okay. Do as they say," Miranda said, pushing on her brother's arm.

"If you're sure. I'll be right outside. Don't leave me, sis. Promise me you'll fight this."

"I will. Now leave."

Tim finally relented and did as requested. Outside, he paced the corridor while running a hand through his unkempt hair. *Please let her survive. I'm nothing without her by my side.*

It seemed like hours before the doctor finally came out of the cubicle. He was smiling which had to be a good sign, didn't it?

"Is she going to be all right?"

"Yes, it would appear you brought her here in time to save her life." He lowered his voice and asked, "Did she tell you why she tried to kill herself?"

Tim shrugged and then pointed to his head. "She's mixed up upstairs. We had a terrible childhood, we were both abused as kids. She can cope with the memories and torment most of the time, but every now and again something triggers and she spirals out of control."

"I'm so sorry to hear that. Has she sought help from a psychiatrist?"

"Dozens over the years, none of them have made a jot of difference. She's booked in to see a new one tomorrow as it happens."

"Maybe it was the pressure of that appointment that forced her to try to take her own life. We'd like to keep her in overnight at least for observation."

Tim's mind raced through the fogginess. *She can't stay here. I can't let her out of my sight. I don't trust her. What if she spills the beans during a nap? What then?* "That won't be necessary, Doc, I can take care of her. Just replace the blood she's lost and we'll get out of your hair."

"She hasn't lost that much, not really, so there will be no need for a transfusion. I would much rather your sister be admitted with us for the next twenty-four hours just to make sure."

Tim nodded, the fear rising and settling in his gut. "If you think that's for the greater good."

"I do. I'll contact the Women's Ward, see if they can fit her in."

"Can I go and sit with her?"

"Yes, by all means. I've arranged for the nurse to make her a cup of tea. Do you want one as well?"

"A coffee would be great, thanks."

"I'll get that sorted for you."

Tim pushed back the curtain and entered the cubicle. His sister was sitting up on the trolley bed, her blue eyes full to the rim with a sadness that tore at his heart. "How are you?"

"Alive. Although I don't want to be."

"Miranda, don't say that."

"Why? It's the truth. What the fuck do I have to live for? We've been guilty of the most heinous crimes imaginable. I can't cope with the fallout from that."

Tim placed a finger to his lips. "Keep your voice down, they'll hear you and call the police."

"Let them. I'm done with this, Tim. Admit it, we were in the wrong."

"I can't. All I wanted to do was make it all right for you. Retribution for the crimes they committed against you."

"I told you, they didn't treat me that bad, not really." Her head lowered, and she mumbled, "I might have embellished the truth a little."

He sprang forward and got in her face. "You did what? Are you telling me they didn't rape you?"

Her chin dipped to her chest, and she shook her head.

"What? Did any of them abuse you either mentally or physically?" he asked in a hushed, frantic tone.

"No, they did nothing. Oh, they might have spoken to me like I was a piece of shit most days, but I gave as good as I got from them."

"But… I did all this because I felt sorry for you. They destroyed your world, that's what you told me."

"I lied. I feel ashamed for saying what I did. I'm sorry, none of this should have happened. The guilt is weighing heavily on my mind now, it's too much for me to handle."

He took a step back and stared at her. His beloved sister, the one person in this life he cared the most about, had deceived him, led him to believe he was doing the right thing killing three men, almost four as there was yet another man on their list. He sucked in a deep breath to prevent the anger burning his chest from erupting. *How could she deceive me like this? How? What have I done?*

Bob barged into Sam's office, his face ruby red with excitement. "You're not going to believe this, we've got a major lead."

"What is it?"

"The car has been picked up on the ANPR cameras in Whitehaven."

Sam shot out of her chair and followed him out of the room. "Where?"

"We're tracking its route now," Bob confirmed.

Liam was frantically flicking through several camera angles on his screen. Sam's raging heart rate triggered sweat to pour out on her forehead.

"Here, he seems to be breaking the speed limit," Liam stated.

"As if he's in a rush to get somewhere. Oh God, please don't tell me they're on their way to kill someone else. Are they both in the vehicle?"

Liam pointed at the image of the Peugeot in the top-right corner. "Two people, one male and the other female."

"They're always together, which is good to know. What about the car in front of them? Could they be chasing some-one, getting ready to strike?"

"It's worth checking," Bob agreed.

"I'll keep my eyes open. Just observing the images we have on the screen, all four vehicles in front are different," Liam confirmed.

"There's always a possibility they're keeping their

distance, ensuring several vehicles are between them and their next target, to avoid being spotted," Sam suggested.

"It's a thought." Bob peered over Liam's shoulder. "She seems out of it. Is she awake or asleep?"

Liam zoomed in on the female passenger on one of the clearer images. "Hmm... hard to tell. Maybe she's resting her eyes."

Sam wasn't so sure. "If I was in the passenger seat and being driven by someone imitating Lewis Hamilton, I would definitely feel some kind of motion sickness."

"I suppose it depends if you have a dicky stomach or not," Bob retorted.

The three of them watched the screen for a few moments longer until the car slowed down at the roundabout.

Sam stamped her foot. "Jesus, they've turned left into the hospital. I bet he's taking her to A and E."

"You could be right. Do you want to get over there?" Bob asked.

"We need to get patrol cars over there ASAP. See if anyone is in the area. They'll get there quicker than we can if they are."

"Leave it with me." Liam picked up the phone to contact the control room.

"Get your jacket, Bob. We'll get on the road."

Her partner didn't need telling twice. She ran back into her office and grabbed her coat. On the way down the stairs, she decided to call into the armoury locker and sign out a Taser, just in case they caught up with the couple. Sam was the only one in their partnership authorised to use the CED (Conducted Energy Devices). Once Sam had signed out the device, they continued out to the car.

Sam used the siren to aid her journey to the hospital. When they arrived, they found three patrol cars located near the entrance to A and E. Sam produced her warrant card. "Have you found anything?"

"The car is parked in the first car park on the right, ma'am," the eldest of the officers replied. "We were unsure what to do next so felt it best to wait here. We were told you were on your way."

"Good, okay, we'll see what we can find out. We're going to need two officers to accompany us, the rest of you man the entrance. Do you know if this is the only way out?"

"Yes, I believe so. All the emergency services enter this way, so I'm guessing it must be," the same officer replied.

"That'll make it easier. Stay vigilant and be aware of your surroundings at all times. Do any of you have Tasers?"

"Yes, two of us. You want us to use them if they try to escape?"

"Play it by ear. We're talking about serial killers here, not just a couple who are guilty of GBH."

"Yes, ma'am. We'll be ready in that case. Taggart and Dance, you'd better remain outside ready to use your equipment, along with me and Adams. Salter and Caldwell, you go with the Inspector."

Sam, Bob and the two uniformed officers entered the hospital. There were two anxious-looking receptionists sitting behind the desk.

Sam flashed her warrant card. "We're searching for two people, a man and a woman. We've had access to camera footage, the woman seemed drowsy. Wait, I have a picture of them here." She scrolled through the recent images on her phone and showed it to the first receptionist who gasped.

"Yes, they came in a while ago. The woman was bleeding. She had cut her wrists in an attempted suicide."

"I see. Where are they now? Is the woman all right?"

"I believe she's been admitted to the Women's Ward. I can call for the doctor to come and see you."

"Yes, please. Just to check, is this the only way out?"

"Yes, apart from the emergency exit at the rear, of course."

"Can you tell us where that is? Is it alarmed?"

"Yes, to both. Go down the corridor on the right and it's just around the corner at the end. We get notified when the door has been opened. The alarm hasn't gone off so far."

Sam smiled at the flustered woman. "Great information. Thank you. Has the man come back to this area at all?"

"No. We've not seen either of them since they were taken through to triage."

"Okay, if we can have a brief word with the doctor first."

The receptionist immediately rang another department, and the doctor who had seen to the suspects appeared moments later.

Sam showed him her ID. "Sorry to disturb you, I appreciate how busy you are. We're looking for a man and a woman. The receptionist has identified the couple and said the woman had tried to commit suicide. Can you tell me when and how she was treated?"

"Indeed. I treated the woman for loss of blood and tended to her wounds around twenty minutes ago. She was then transferred to the ward and ordered to stay overnight. Her brother went with her."

"And their names?"

"Her name is Miranda Wallace," the doctor confirmed. "Sorry, that's all I can tell you. I need to get back to triage now."

"I understand. Thank you for your time, Doctor."

The doctor hurried back from where he came, and the receptionist gasped. "Should I ring the Women's Ward, you know, to warn them?"

"No, we'll head up there now. What floor is it?"

"Third floor, right at the end of the corridor. You won't do anything risky, will you?"

Sam smiled reassuringly at the woman. "Not if it can be avoided. Don't worry."

Sam spotted the lift in the corner. She instructed Salter to guard the fire exit, and Caldwell accompanied her and Bob up to the third floor.

Before the doors opened, Sam withdrew her weapon. "I hope I don't have to use it, but I will if I deem it necessary."

"I'd zap the bastard as soon as I laid eyes on him," Bob mumbled.

Sam dug him in the ribs. "Maybe it's just as well you're not registered to use one."

The doors *swooshed* open, and the three of them exited the lift, cautiously keeping a watchful eye for movement during their journey up the corridor.

Sam applied the antibacterial gel at the door and entered the ward with the weapon still drawn down by her side. A pretty blonde nurse approached her.

"Hello, can I help?" Her gaze dropped to the weapon.

Sam placed a finger to her lips to silence the woman. "We're the police." Bob thrust his ID at the nurse. "We're after a Miranda Wallace, is she here?"

"Yes. She's got the curtain pulled around the bed."

"Is she alone?"

"Yes. Her brother has just left the ward. I think he went in search of the loo or possibly to get himself a drink."

"Okay. We're here to arrest the pair of them. Can you help us?"

The nurse looked horrified by the suggestion and raised her hands. "Does it have to be here? We have seriously sick people on this ward. Can't you arrest him outside, in the corridor?"

The nurse made a valid point.

"Yes, okay. Would it be all right if I left the uniformed

officer with Miranda? The last thing we need is for her to take flight."

"Okay, that seems to be a suitable compromise."

Sam turned to Caldwell. "Go and sit with Miranda. Tell her she's under arrest and she'll only make matters worse if she causes a fuss."

"Will do, ma'am."

Sam and Bob left the ward. A man walked towards them. His gaze met Sam's, and he turned and ran.

"Shit! It's him."

She and Bob sprinted after him. He burst through a door, and they upped their pace as he disappeared out of sight.

"First opportunity you get, zap the bastard," Bob suggested.

"Don't worry about me, I'll do it when I see fit. There might be too many people around, it seems busy here today."

"Hospitals are always busy."

They barged through the door, almost knocking over an elderly man with a walking frame.

"'Ere, watch what you're doing. This isn't a children's playground, you know. Shame on you!"

"Sorry. It's an emergency. Did you see in which direction the man who came through the doors before us went?"

He pointed behind him. "Down there, door on the right."

"Thank you." Sam held the door open for the man.

He waddled slowly past her. She soon regretted her decision. Bob gritted his teeth and pulled a face behind the man's back. Sam let the door go once the man was safely through it.

"Don't say anything, I'm far too polite for my own good. Come on."

They raced down the hallway and stopped outside the door.

"It's a storeroom," Sam said. "Be on your guard. This will probably be the only way in and out."

"You just worry about yourself. Don't forget you're the one holding the zapper."

Sam shook her head, her patience fading with her partner's attitude. "Ready?"

"Yep. Go for it." Bob kicked open the door. It slammed against the wall behind. "Come out, Wallace, we know you're in here."

They were presuming his name was Wallace after what the receptionist and doctor had told them back in A and E.

"Fuck off. Come any closer and you won't know what's hit you."

"Show yourself," Sam ordered. "There's no way out. We have you cornered. Your sister has already been arrested. The game is up."

"Don't bullshit me. I'll go down fighting, you're nuts if you think I won't."

"We're aware of the crimes you've committed and the violence you're capable of. I will have no hesitation in using the Taser if I'm forced to. I'm telling you now to come out and surrender, either that or suffer the consequences. All of this could be avoided with you showing yourself."

"Bollocks. It takes guts to hurt someone with one of those things. Most coppers don't have what it takes."

"You're right, they're only handed out to well-trained officers; some pause longer than necessary to give the suspect the chance to make the right decision. The choice is yours. I want to assure you, though, I've only been forced to draw a Taser three times throughout my career and I've never hesitated once in using it."

"Fuck off if you think I'm falling for that one."

"Have the guts to come out without us using excessive force to arrest you. We don't intend backing down."

"We appear to be at an impasse then because I have no intention of backing down either."

"I repeat, the choice is yours, Wallace."

The suspect fell silent. Sam knew he was probably mulling over the options he had in front of him. Suddenly, he appeared. Sam held her weapon firmly with both hands.

Wallace immediately put his hands up. "All right. I'll come with you."

"Walk towards me, slowly. Keep your hands where I can see them or I'll fire."

Wallace took three steps forward and stopped. His gaze drifted off to the left at the shelves a few feet away from him. Sam anticipated what his intention was and fired her Taser. The wires sank into his chest, and he dropped to his knees then tipped backwards to lie flat on the floor, his body juddering with the surge running through him. Sam released her finger, and together, she and Bob, raced forward to arrest the suspect. Bob slapped his cuffs on Wallace and hauled him to his feet.

Wallace was subdued on the way back to the car, didn't even ask how his sister was and what was going to happen to her.

As soon as they arrived at the station, Sam contacted Jackie Penrose to cancel the press conference that had been arranged for that afternoon. There was no point going ahead with it now the suspects were in custody. She also arranged with the desk sergeant for a uniformed officer to remain by Miranda's side until she was released from hospital. With everything now covered and with Wallace banged up in a cell, Sam returned to the incident room. The team applauded her entrance.

She waved away their congratulations and headed over to make a coffee. "I'm in dire need of caffeine, anyone else?"

Bob helped to distribute the drinks. "Are we going to question him today or let him stew overnight?"

"I'd rather get it done and dusted today. Do you have any plans for this evening?"

"None that can't be postponed." He glanced up at the clock on the wall. "It's three o'clock now, we should be done by around six at the latest, shouldn't we?"

"I admire your optimism. It depends if he's willing to cooperate or not."

"You could always threaten to zap him again."

The room erupted into laughter. It felt good for Sam to relieve at least a small portion of the stress clawing at her shoulders. She spent the next thirty minutes making notes, preparing herself for the important interview ahead of her. But before she went downstairs, she rang Vernon.

"Hi, it's me. We've just arrested two suspects. I have to interview one before I can think about coming home tonight. Sorry to put you out, but I hope you don't mind looking after Sonny for a while longer?"

"No problem. Any idea how long you're likely to be or is that a daft question?"

"Not daft, just one I don't have an answer to. I'll ring when I'm on my way, how's that?"

"Okay, I may be speaking out of turn, not running this past Crystal first, but why don't you stay here tonight? I've cobbled together a curry, it'll stretch to three, if you're up for it?"

"That would be wonderful. What would I do without you guys?"

"It's what family are for. Take care, Sam. Don't worry about Sonny, he's fast asleep in front of the fire. I've worn him out."

"I can visualise the scene. Bless him, I'll make it up to him tomorrow, or when I get back later."

"See you soon. Good luck with the rest of your day."

"Thanks, Vernon." She had such a lot to tell him and her

sister later, if she had the energy left to fill them in. Inhaling a deep breath in preparation, she picked up her notes and collected her partner on the way through the incident room.

"Is the duty solicitor here yet, Nick?" she asked the desk sergeant.

"She's about two minutes away, ma'am."

The door opened, and in walked a leggy blonde Sam had dealt with in the past, Donna Jordache.

"Shit!" Bob cursed beside her. He turned and faced the wall. Sam thought his behaviour was odd. Is there something going on between him and Donna? Surely not, he would have told me. Wouldn't he?

"What's wrong?" she asked out of the corner of her mouth.

"I'll tell you later. Just ignore me."

"That's a little hard, partner. If there's something I should know before we go in there, tell me now."

"There's not. I'll tell you later," he repeated, sounding agitated.

"I can do without you pissing me off, bearing in mind what lies ahead of us."

"Sorry. Just ignore me."

"I intend to." She turned away from her partner and welcomed the solicitor. "Ah, Miss Jordache, nice of you to join us. Do you want to see your client first?"

"Thanks, if I could have five minutes with him?"

"Of course. Bob, can you collect Mr Wallace and bring him to the interview room?"

"On it now."

Sam gestured for Donna Jordache to join her, and they made their way down the hallway to Interview Room One at the bottom. "Can I get you a drink?"

"No, thanks. I have a bottle of water with me if I need it."

"Of course you do. You're aware of the charges we're bringing against Mr Wallace, I take it?"

"Three counts of murder, so I understand. Have you got the proof to back up your allegations?"

"I do, otherwise we wouldn't have charged him. I know the procedures, Miss Jordache."

"I have no doubt about that, Inspector," the solicitor said spikily.

Sam left the room. Bob was on his way down the corridor with the cuffed suspect. Wallace had his head bowed. Sam wondered if he was remorseful about the murders he had committed or the fact that he'd been caught. She opened the door and left him with the solicitor and a uniformed officer standing at the back of the room.

Once the door had closed behind the suspect, Sam asked, "Are you going to tell me what's going on?"

Bob shuffled his feet. "I can't. Not yet."

"This doesn't make sense, Bob. Look at me when I'm speaking to you. You're making me ruddy nervous."

Bob glanced her way but quickly averted his gaze.

"Shit! Shit! Shit! I know what's going on. Fuck it. Is she the one?"

Her partner's eyes closed, and his chest inflated. After a few seconds, he confirmed what she'd been dreading to hear. "Yes. She was the one waving and blowing kisses at Chris this morning."

Sam faced the wall, rested her forehead against it and then kicked it a few times. "Bloody hell. I wish you hadn't told me. Now I have to face her across the table, knowing that she's been shagging my husband behind my back."

Bob placed a hand on her shoulder. "You forced it out of me. I'm sorry, I had no intention of telling you until the interview was over."

"That's it, blame me. That's all you men like to do, blame us women, even when we're not in the wrong."

"I'm sorry, Sam. I promise, if it could have been avoided…"

"I'll be right back. I need to nip to the loo." She propelled herself off the wall, ran up the corridor and back up the stairs. There she found Claire in the ladies', washing her hands at the sink.

"Everything all right, boss? You look a bit peaky."

"I'm fine. I think. I just need to take five minutes to gather my thoughts, thanks, Claire."

"I'll leave you to it." Claire smiled and walked out of the door.

Sam stared at her reflection, long and hard. She wasn't that bad-looking, certainly nothing in comparison to Donna Jordache, but she had a good heart. *What am I thinking? This is about Chris's needs, not my failings.* She gave herself a good talking-to and went back downstairs.

"Are you still speaking to me?" Bob whispered.

Sam smiled. "I am. It wasn't your fault. You did your best to protect me. Come on, bitch, let's get this interview over with."

Bob chuckled. "You tell her."

The door opened, and the uniformed officer asked Sam and Bob to come in.

Bob made the obligatory speech to the recording equipment, and the interview got underway. Sam wasn't surprised when Wallace went down the 'no comment' route. It was the way of the world, apparently. Every solicitor worth their salt always advised their client to spout those two notorious words.

"We have the evidence in the form of fingerprints at two of the scenes, and at the third we have a pretty conclusive tyre track that we'll be matching to your vehicle. Hard to discount that amount of evidence, wouldn't you agree, Mr Wallace?"

"No comment," he replied, dipping his head once more.

"And then there's the photographic evidence to consider. We have you drinking at the pub with victim one, Brian Coltman. Any reason you chose a different identity? You went under the name of Ian whilst befriending the man, if I'm not mistaken."

"No comment."

"All right. Tell me this, if you will: why were the men targeted?"

"No comment." Wallace shuffled uncomfortably in his seat.

Sam watched his movements through narrowed eyes. When she didn't ask another question, his gaze met hers.

"What?" he said.

"Let's try again, shall we? Why were the three victims targeted?"

He remained silent and studied the desk in front of her.

"Why don't I tell you what I think? It's to do with your sister, am I right?"

His head shot up, and his gaze seared into hers. "No comment."

"What were they? Men she had fallen for and they'd dumped her? Or men she had fantasised about and they wanted nothing to do with her?"

He shook his head.

"So why did Miranda attempt to take her own life today? Guilt? Because she couldn't handle the guilt of seeing the men lose their lives? Go on, admit it, I'm right, aren't I?"

"Leave her out of this. It was all down to me, it has nothing to do with her."

Sam clenched her hands on the table. "I wish I could. The trouble is, we have footage disputing what you're telling me.

How else can you explain your sister being covered in your third victim's blood? She was also the prime participant in the honeytrap, too, wasn't she? If that's what it was."

"It wasn't… I mean, no comment."

Sam refused to back down. She spent the next two hours repeating the same questions over and over, which led to Tim repeating the same two annoying words in response.

Until Donna Jordache reached for her bottle of water and cleared her throat. "Shall we move on? My client has no intention of saying anything other than 'no comment'."

"As per your advice, no doubt," Sam snapped back.

Jordache's eyes widened and then narrowed a few times. "Moving on, Inspector," she repeated.

"I agree. I think we're through here. We have enough evidence to charge you and we'll be interviewing your sister soon enough. By the sounds of it, the guilt is weighing heavily on her shoulders. From experience, I know where that can lead."

"I want to be there during the interview," Jordache pitched in.

"I'll be sure to let the duty sergeant know. Of course, there's every possibility that Miss Wallace will insist on going it alone, without a solicitor present."

"I'll do my very best to ensure that doesn't happen, Inspector."

"I have no doubts there. We're done. If you can wind up the proceedings for me, DS Jones." Sam rose from her chair and left the room. She was halfway along the corridor when a voice called her name.

"Inspector, a word with you before you go, if I may?"

She turned around to find Donna Jordache waiting for her, her arms crossed and wearing an expression not dissimilar to that of someone having to contend with a stormy weekend. "What was that in there?"

"You tell me. I have three bodies lying in the mortuary after being sliced up by this couple, and you instruct your client to go down the 'no comment' route."

"He'll have his day in court. Like all the other criminals out there."

"He will. I'll make sure of it. I'll also get the victims' families the justice they deserve. How do you sleep at night, Ms Jordache?"

"Not bad. You?"

"Oh yes, a sound night's sleep is always a good indication of a clear conscience."

Jordache frowned. "Is that statement supposed to mean something?"

Sam shrugged. "Oh, and by the way, you might want to tell that scum of a husband of mine that I've changed the locks, so he won't be able to sneak back into my home again in my absence. Good luck with your budding romance, you're going to need it." She watched the colour drain from the solicitor's face, turned on her heel and marched up the corridor. *Put that in your fucking sexy bodice, love.*

At the top of the stairs, Sam let out the breath she'd been holding in and punched the air.

EPILOGUE

The next day proved to be far more interesting than Sam could have ever anticipated. First, Miranda had requested Sam's attendance at the hospital, where she had no hesitation revealing the facts about all three murders. Miranda was full of remorse, unlike her brother. Sam had the feeling, that given the chance, if the suspect wasn't on a twenty-four-hour watch, she would willingly have attempted to end her life again.

Ultimately, the brother and sister were charged with the three murders. Her brother was sent to prison on remand, and they found his sister a bed in the nearest high security hospital. Sam was eager to ensure she didn't try to commit suicide before the victims' families had their day in court. After that, in her opinion, Miranda could do what she frigging liked.

After she had verbally slapped Jordache down in the corridor, Sam had finally received a call from her missing husband. An irate one at that. He had threatened all sorts. She had listened to him ranting, losing his rag, with a composure she never knew she possessed. Then, after his angry tirade had dried up, she ordered him to never ring or contact her again and gave him the name of her solicitor. That stunned him into silence, then she hit him where it really hurt.

"You will regret the day you ever slept with that woman behind my back, Chris. Don't think you'll get your hands on half the proceeds of the house either because you saw to it that every loan we took out was in my name. I have news for you, I'll make sure my solicitor reclaims the money for those loans from any money owing to you. Furthermore, I will impress upon my solicitor that you emotionally blackmailed me into signing those papers."

A few huffy breaths from his end, and then he hung up without uttering another word. What else could he say?

With Chris and all his selfish behaviour now in the past, she was looking forward to her first date with Rhys. Instead of meeting him at his office as they had arranged, she had switched plans and invited him to come to the house instead. Insisting he should bring Benji with him. She prepared one of the best meals she'd ever made for any man. In her mind, that reinforced the fact that she was doing the right thing being with him.

She welcomed them both with a glass of wine for Rhys and a bowl of water for Benji. He and Sonny ran the length of the house for the next ten minutes until they were exhausted and had flaked out under the kitchen table.

Sam and Rhys clinked their glasses together. It was then that Rhys revealed something that rocked her to the core.

Holding eye contact with her, he exhaled a large breath and said, "I wasn't going to tell you this, but here goes."

Sam's heart raced. Oh shit! Don't spoil everything by telling me you're married.

He smiled. "Don't look so worried. It's to do with work."

"Phew, I thought all this was going to end before it had really started."

He reached for her hand and grasped it tightly. "Don't be silly. Okay, I need you to remain calm while I tell you this, promise me?"

"How can I promise that if I don't know what you're going to say?"

He laughed. "Nevertheless, I need you to promise me."

She puffed out her cheeks and nodded. "You have my word. Hit me with it."

"It's to do with your last investigation. The brother and sister serial killers."

Sam took a sip from her glass. "Go on, what about them?"

"She was due to see me this evening."

"What? Professionally?"

"Yes. You remember I told you that I had a new client seeking my help? It was her."

She took several more sips from her wine. "How do you know?"

"Her name. I recognised the name Miranda when you told me you'd caught them. I spoke to her brother who sought out my advice and made the appointment. He clearly cares about her."

"Yeah, I suppose he must do if he was prepared to kill for her. Oh God, what if she had come to you and...?"

"And? You think that might have put me in danger?"

Sam shrugged and heaved out a breath. "Who knows? If you'd seen her and given her the wrong advice... no, I don't want to contemplate the consequences."

"It's better if we don't dwell on the ifs and maybes. Let's just be grateful that you caught them when you did. Have I told you how amazing you are?"

The heat rose in her cheeks, and it wasn't from the alcohol

she'd downed either. "Thank you. My team and I always work hard. Although saying that, I think this couple made it easy for us along the way. The truth is, I still believe they committed the murders with the intention of getting caught."

"Hard to fathom out what goes on in people's heads, trust me, I should know. Anyway, let's put work aside for now and concentrate on our future." He raised his glass. "To us."

Sam smiled, feeling the happiest she'd felt in years. "To us and our future."

They chinked glasses again, then Rhys left his chair and came to stand in front of her. He held out his hands. She put hers in his, and he helped her to her feet. Then they shared a kiss that took her breath away, leaving her in no doubt that she was doing the right thing getting involved with him.

THE END

THANK you for reading another adventure in the DI Sam Cobbs series, book four, To Prove Fatal is now available.

MAYBE YOU'D ALSO LIKE to try one of my other edge-of-your-seat thriller series. Grab the first book in the best-selling, award-winning Justice series here, Cruel Justice.

OR THE FIRST book in the spin-off Justice Again series, Gone In Seconds.

OR MY OTHER super successful police procedural series set in Hereford. Find the first book in the DI Sara Ramsey series, No Right to Kill

PERHAPS YOU'D PREFER to try one of my other police procedural series, the DI Kayli Bright series which begins with The Missing Children.

OR MAYBE YOU'D enjoy the DI Sally Parker series set in Norfolk, Wrong Place.

OR MY GRITTY police procedural starring DI Nelson set in Manchester, Torn Apart.

OR MY BEST-SELLING psychological thriller _She's Gone._

KEEP IN TOUCH WITH M A COMLEY

Twitter
http://twitter.com/ComleyMel

Blog
http://melcomley.blogspot.com

Facebook
Readers' Group

Newsletter
http://smarturl.it/8jtcvv

BookBub
www.bookbub.com/authors/m-a-comley

Printed in Great Britain
by Amazon

57307084R00126